INTERIM SITE

M/   8

/
J

S

/

[

JL   )

SIXTEEN

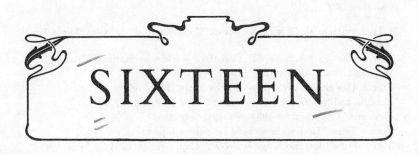

SIXTEEN

Short Stories

by

Outstanding Writers

for Young Adults

Edited by

DONALD R. GALLO

Delacorte Press
New York

Published by
Delacorte Press
1 Dag Hammarskjold Plaza
New York, N.Y. 10017

A portion of this book's royalties, earmarked for research in young-adult literature, will go to the National Council of Teachers of English.

Manufactured in the United States of America

Book Design by Bente Hamann

First printing

Library of Congress Cataloging in Publication Data
Main entry under title:

Sixteen: short stories by outstanding young adult writers.

Summary: Sixteen short stories, dealing with teenage concerns, written especially for this collection by well-known authors of young adult novels such as the Mazers, M. E. Kerr, Robert Cormier, Bette Greene, and Richard Peck. Biographical sketches of each author are included, as well as follow-up activities for the reader.

[1. Short stories] I. Gallo, Donald R. II. Title: 16.
PZ5.S619   1984   [Fic]
ISBN 0-385-29346-1
Library of Congress Catalog Card Number: 84–3250

For B, C, and D

ABOUT THE EDITOR

Donald R. Gallo is Professor of English at Central Connecticut State University, where he teaches courses in writing and in literature for young adults. He is a former junior high school English teacher and reading specialist and former editor of the *Connecticut English Journal,* and his publications include materials for teaching reading and literature, as well as numerous articles and reviews in professional books and journals. He lives in Cromwell, Connecticut.

ACKNOWLEDGMENTS

For their enthusiasm and continued encouragement throughout this project, my thanks go to authors Robin F. Brancato, Robert Cormier, Bette Greene, Norma Klein, Walter Dean Myers, and Richard Peck as well as to paperback wholesaler Allan Hartley who fanned the initial sparks.

For reading and commenting on a variety of these stories, thanks go to Connecticut teachers Connie Aloise, Phil Connors, Ed Flynn, Gil Hunt, Ellen Stankevich, and Chris Sullivan and their students at Bloomfield Junior High School, J. F. Kennedy Junior High School in Enfield, Wilcox Vocational Technical High School in Meriden, Manchester High School, Cromwell Middle School, and Plainville High School.

My special thanks to Chris Archacki for her enduring interest, perceptive analyses, candid advice, and unabashed joy in reading.

D. Gallo

INTRODUCTION

This book you now hold is unique—in two ways. First, there has never before been a collection of short stories written specifically for teen-agers by authors who specialize in writing books for young people. Second, none of these stories has appeared in print before, except for one that appeared in a now defunct magazine in a slightly different form. Thus they are all new stories and they were written and assembled here just for you.

Almost all of the short stories in anthologies used in schools today, or that are available in bookstores or libraries, were written by authors who usually write for adults, even though some of those stories—like John Updike's "A&P"—may have teen-agers as main characters. Or they are collections of world-famous stories now considered classics, like Jack London's "To Build a Fire."

In contrast, contemporary teen-agers and preteen-agers everywhere have been avidly reading novels about young people that were written especially for them by a number of well-known authors. Some of those authors, such as Joan Aiken, Robert Cormier, and Norma Fox Mazer, also write and publish short stories for teen-agers. So we asked them, along with nearly thirty other respected and well-known writers of young adult novels, to write a short story for this collection. We selected the sixteen best stories from those we received, and we arranged them under several headings that indicate something of the focus of their content: Friendships, Turmoils, Loves, Decisions, and Families.

These are stories about young people from twelve to eighteen. Most are realistic stories, while three are fantasy or science fiction. Teen-age concerns and problems are the focus of most of them, though parents and a teacher figure prominently in some of them.

You will find stories about hope and hate and love and death here. Some of them will make you laugh. One or two might raise a tear in your eye or at least a lump in your throat. You will identify with the problems—or perhaps recognize yourself—in some of these stories, though you probably will be glad you don't have to exchange places with some of the characters.

Because there is a wide variety of topics and styles in this collection, you may find some stories you don't like. That's normal. The same thing would happen if you tried everything on a restaurant menu. But you may also find several stories that you will not only like but that you will also want to read again and again and share with your friends and your parents.

If you like a particular story and want to read something else by the same author, we have provided a list and a brief description of each author's books as part of a biographical sketch following each story.

In addition, in the back of the book you will find a few questions to think about or to discuss with other readers after you have finished reading. We have made a few suggestions for writing, too. We hope that both types of activities will help you delve deeper into the stories and then to go beyond them with your own ideas and experiences.

Finally, we hope that these stories will entertain and challenge you—after all, this book is for you.

CONTENTS

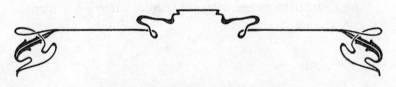

FRIENDSHIPS

Times are tough. Unemployment is high. Food is scarce. Hannah is a kid with a growling stomach, but she's just discovered a clever way to satisfy her hunger. . . .

I, HUNGRY HANNAH CASSANDRA GLEN . . .

NORMA FOX MAZER

When Mr. Augustus Francher's heart burst, I told Crow we were going to the service at Bascind's Funeral Home because, afterward, at Mrs. Francher's house, there would be food.

"How are we supposed to get in? Nobody asked us," he said.

"They will. First we go to the service—to show respect, you know. Mrs. Francher sees us there and she says, 'You two fine young people must come over to my house after the funeral and have some delicious food.'"

"Safety Pin Francher says that? Wake up, Hannah dreamer."

"Maybe she won't say it exactly that way," I admitted.

"Maybe she won't," Crow mocked. "Forget it. I don't want to go." He scraped his Adidas on the curb.

"You never want to go anywhere." Just because of his face. He had to go to school, he couldn't get out of that, but he didn't like to go anyplace else where there were a lot of people.

"You go," he said.

"Not without you." We went everywhere together. We had been friends since we were four years old. "Just think of all that food," I urged Crow. "I bet there'll be those little tiny fancy hot dogs with toothpicks stuck in them.

You know how good they smell? And a baked ham stuck all over with cloves and slices of pineapple on top. There's got to be a cake—maybe a three-layer chocolate cake with chocolate icing—and ice cream and tons of cookies. She's got the whole store to choose from."

I talked about food until Crow couldn't stand it. "I'll go, I'll go, since you want to do it so much."

"Just for me. Big-hearted you."

Crow was always hungry. His elbows stuck out like sticks. His stepfather, Willie, was on half time at the Buffalo Chemical Works, but even when he was on full time and they had more money, Crow was hungry.

Willie said workingmen had to get fed first. (That was Willie.) Then, said Willie, came the littlest kids, Jay, Mike, Chris, and Kelly. After that came the women—Crow's mother and Willie's two daughters, Lisa and Janet. After that, said Willie, came older boys. That was Crow. His mom always saved him something, but he never got enough to eat.

In the funeral parlor, we signed our names in the guest book. David James Alpern. Hannah C. Glen. We followed two men into the chapel and Crow sat down in the last row. If there'd been a darkest corner, he would have chosen that. I sat down next to him.

In the front row, Mrs. Francher sniffled loudly. She was tall and shaped like a summer squash, skinny on top and swelling out on the bottom. In the store she always wore a dark green smock held together with safety pins. Today she had on a black dress and black hat, no safety pins anywhere in sight.

Crow's stomach rumbled and then mine did, like a two-piece band. "What'd you have for breakfast?" I whispered. He shrugged. I had had two grape jelly sandwiches and a glass of instant milk. After she got laid off at the paper-bag factory, my mother began buying powdered milk instead of whole milk. She said it was cheaper and just as good for us. Every day she went out looking for work. As soon as she found a job, we'd have real milk again and plenty of eggs. At night, instead of macaroni and cheese, we'd have hamburgers that sizzled delicious-smelling fat all over the stove and vegetables cooked with hunks of margarine. And for dessert we'd have cookies and freestone peaches in thick syrup.

A man wearing a peppermint-striped tie passed us and then came back. I thought he was going to say something about Crow. Once, on a bus, a man said in a loud voice to the woman with him that Crow's parents should do something about his face. Mostly, people just stared.

"You, young lady," Peppermint Tie said, "shouldn't be chewing gum in here."

I spit the gum out into my hand. As soon as Peppermint Tie went by I put it up under my upper lip to save for later. Crow said it made him hungrier to chew gum. It was just the opposite for me.

Sometimes I thought that if Crow didn't have that stuff on his face he would be prettier than a girl. He had high cheekbones and his eyes were dark and shining, but it was hard to notice because his face looked as if it had been splashed with gobs of rusty paint. A splash like a map of Tennessee covered half his forehead, wandered down over his left eye, and dribbled out onto his cheek. Another splash around his mouth and chin looked like a mushy baked apple, and a splash on his neck looked like a four-legged spider.

A minister came into the chapel from a side door and stood near the open coffin. He cleared his throat. "Good afternoon, friends." He began talking about Mr. Francher. "Augustus Francher has left us. He was a fine, upstanding man."

No, I thought, that's wrong. He was a fine man, but he didn't stand up any more than he had to. Mr. Francher was fat, his face was round and yellow as a lemon pie, and he wheezed when he talked. If he and Mrs. Francher were both in the store, she waited on the customers and Mr. Francher sat on a high stool in front of the cash register. He always wore big soft shoes, a white shirt with a little bow tie, and baggy black pants.

"He lived a good life," the minister said. "He had charity in his heart and we are saddened that he has been struck down in his prime." Mrs. Francher sniffled loudly and called out, "Oh, Augustus, Augustus."

Mr. and Mrs. Francher's grocery store was in the front of their house. Dried salamis hung in the window over dusty stacks of Campbell's baked beans and Diet Pepsi. Lots of mornings when Crow and I walked past on the way to school, Mr. Francher's round yellow face would be in the window, between the salamis, and he would wink at me.

At the end of the month when my mom was short of money, she'd send me to Francher's Groceteria for half a pound of bologna and a can of spaghetti for supper. "Tell Francher to put it on the bill, Hanny," she'd say.

And I'd go off, hoping and hoping that it would be Mr. Francher in the store. If it was Mrs. Francher, she'd finger a safety pin on her smock, click her tongue, and look up what we owed in her account book. "Twenty-five dollars and seventy-six cents. You'd better pay something on that." And she'd hold out her hand as if I had money in my pocket. I would try not to look at the tub of creamy-looking potato salad in the case or the round of cheese on the counter with the sharp cheese knife lying next to it. "Go home and see what your mother wants to pay on account," she'd order.

But if it was Mr. Francher, he'd put his hand on my shoulder, look right at me with his brown eyes that were bright as a chipmunk's, and say, "Now, daughter, just tell your mother not to forget she should pay up soon." And he'd pull the can of spaghetti down from the shelf. Once he'd told me that long ago he'd had a little sister who died, and her name, too, was Hannah. "A nice old-fashioned name," he said. He was shorter than his wife and, sitting on his stool, he would munch on cream-filled doughnuts, then wash them down with long sips from a bottle of soda. My mother said he was his own best customer.

The minister was through talking about Mr. Francher and everybody stood up to walk around the coffin where he lay, wearing a dark suit and tie, his hands folded together over his big round stomach. I stopped in surprise. He looked like a baby in a crib, a huge baby who would, at any moment, open his eyes and chuckle. His cheeks were puffed out and shining.

Mrs. Francher stood off to one side with another woman, also in black. They were holding hands. I walked slowly past the coffin, looking back at Mr. Francher over my shoulder. Was he really gone? Was it true that when I went to Francher's the next time, there would be no Mr. Francher to say, "Now, daughter . . ."? No Mr. Francher anymore to wink at me through the salamis? My eyes filled. Just then I understood that he was dead and what it meant.

Behind me, Crow jabbed his finger into my back, reminding me why we were there. "Mrs. Francher," I said. Her eyes were dark and puffy. She looked at me, through me. I didn't think she recognized me.

It was the other woman who answered. "Yes?" She was not as tall as Mrs. Francher, but she was shaped the same: summer squash. "What is it, dear?" she said. "What do you want?"

"I—can we—I'm sorry about Mr. Francher," I said. "I wish—I'm *sorry.*"

Mrs. Francher's eyes focused. "You're the Glen girl." She reached up to the neck of her dress and a glimmer of surprise (that there was no safety pin there?) seemed to cross her face. I thought she was going to ask when my mother would pay up.

And fast, not so brave now that I was face-to-face with her, I said, "Can we, can Crow and—can David and I come after the funeral to your house?"

She grabbed my arm and bent close to me. "You came to the service. I didn't know you loved him so much."

I nodded dumbly. She smelled of chocolate mints and mothballs.

"And him?" Flapping her hand in Crow's direction, she looked away from him, but the other woman stared.

A man reached past me and pressed Mrs. Francher's shoulder. "My sympathies, Berenice."

"Thank you, Jack. Do you know my sister? This is my sister, Celia. Come to the house," she said. "You're coming to the house after, aren't you?"

"We'll be there," he said. "Jane made a meat pie."

"Move on, dear, move on," Mrs. Francher's sister said. She was all in black, too. "People are waiting. Move, children."

My mouth watered. A meat pie! "Thank you, we'll come to your house," I said, sort of low and fast, as we walked by Mrs. Francher and her sister.

Outside, cars with headlights on were lined up for the drive to the cemetery. Mrs. Francher and her sister got into Bascind's long black limousine. A chauffeur with a black peaked cap drove.

"I'm not going to die the way old Francher did," Crow said as we walked down the street. "I'm not going to wait around for it to come get me. When I'm ready, I'm going to do it myself."

"You mean kill yourself?"

He nodded. "I've thought about it a lot. I might do it soon."

"Soon? Now that is truly dumb. I never heard anything so magnifico dumb."

"Give me one good reason."

"I'll give you ten good reasons. You're too young. You don't know what you're saying. You get these ideas in your head and you think they mean something. Sometimes you make me so mad!"

"Now there's a good reason."

"Besides," I said coldly, "it's against the law."

"Oh, dear, dear, dear. I forgot that. After I stick my

head in the oven some night, they're going to arrest my corpse and send it to jail for life."

"Would you please knock it off! I don't want you dead. So just forget it."

"Even if I leave you my track shoes?" He held up a foot temptingly.

"Oh, your brothers would get them."

"I'll make a will," he said. "I'll leave them to you in my will."

We sat on the stoop in front of my house where we could watch down the block to see when Mrs. Francher arrived back from the cemetery.

"Go get us some paper and pencils," Crow said.

"You want to play tic-tac-toe? Again?" It was his favorite game and no wonder, he always won.

"I'm going to write my will. You can do yours, too. Everybody should have a will."

"Not kids."

"Who says? Putting my track shoes in my will makes it official. You get them, nobody else."

"I don't want your track shoes, and I don't want to make a will. I'm not going to die."

"Well, not right away," he agreed. "But you never know. I bet Mr. Francher didn't think he was going to drop dead. Give me your key, I'll go in and get the stuff if you're too lazy."

"You are one magnifico pest." I went into the apartment, tore paper out of my notebook, and grabbed two pencil stubs from the coffee tin in the kitchen. I didn't want to use up my ball-point pen.

"Make sure you leave me something good," Crow said when I sat down next to him again. He smoothed out his piece of paper on his knee.

"This is dumb," I said. Crow was already scribbling away. "I don't even know how to start."

"Don't be difficult, Hanny." He held up his paper and read out, " 'I, David James Alpern, being of exceptionally sound mind and not so good body, do hereby make my last

will and testament.' That's the way you begin. That's all
there is to it. Then 'I leave to etcetera, etcetera.' "

After a while, I wrote. "I, the hungry Hannah Cassandra
Glen, being of possibly sound mind and passably sound
body, do hereby make my last will. I leave—"

But I couldn't think of anything I had that anyone
would want. No, that was a lie. I didn't want to give my
things away. I fingered the string of blue coral around my
neck and thought of the green and white afghan on my
bed, which my grandmother had made years before for
my mother. It always somehow made me think of a spring
day. I had never told anyone that, not even Crow. Then
there were the six little glass chicks that my father had
sent me when I was five, the last thing he ever sent me.
The chicks sometimes marched across the top of my bureau, bumping into the jam jar in which I kept barrettes,
shoelaces, and rubber bands, and sometimes made a
magic circle on the floor at the side of my bed where I
could see them as soon as I woke.

I peered over Crow's shoulder. He had just left an extra
toilet plunger to his stepfather. I thought about putting
down that I left a terrifico job making magnifico money
(maybe as a private secretary to a very important person)
to my mother. "Aren't you done yet?" I asked.

"In a minute." He kept writing and crossing out and
writing.

My stomach rumbled. What if Mrs. Francher and her
sister wouldn't let us in? *No way, you kids, all you want is
food, you don't care about poor Mr. Francher being dead.*

I cleaned my fingernails and cuffed up the bottom of my
Levis. They were my best pair. My mother had found
them in a church rummage sale. "Not even worn at the
knees, Hanny!"

Crow turned over his paper to write on the other side.
"Anyone would think you're serious about this," I said.

"I am." He covered his paper with his arm. "No peeking. I'll read it to you when I'm done."

I wrote down that I left Crow my afghan, but I crossed it

out. How could I give that up? I was ashamed of my greediness and willed him my glass chicks. He probably wouldn't even like them.

Finally he stopped writing. "Okay. *Fini.*"

"What now?" I said. "You get out there in traffic and let a car run over you so I can get your track shoes?"

"I wouldn't do it that way. It's not sure enough. Let me tell you, when I do it, I'm not botching it up."

"Read me your will or shut up."

"I, David James Alpern (aka Crow)," he read, "being of exceptionally sound mind and not so good body, leave to my best friend, Hannah Glen, my mighty brain, including all the words she doesn't know—"

"Thanks a lot."

"—a lifetime supply of Tootie Frooty gum—"

"Gimme a break!"

He stopped reading. "Are you going to listen?"

"I'll listen, I'll listen."

"—lifetime supply of Tootie Frooty gum and my track shoes. To my mother, *M*A*S*H* reruns forever and a quiet day. An extra toilet plunger to my stepfather, Willie. To my brothers, Jay and Mike, snot-free noses—shut up please so people can sleep!—birthdays at Burger King, and a snow shovel so you can make some money in the winter. To my sisters, Kelly and Chris, all the tangerines y'all want, a box full of chocolate chip cookies that never goes empty, and Wonder Woman tee shirts, red for Kelly, green for Chris. To Lisa and Janet, getting out of the house safe, thanks for the sandwich under the door, and winning all their volleyball games. And finally to all those others, teachers, acquaintances, enemies, and strangers, good good goodby, y'all, I'm not sorry to leave."

He glanced at me, the way he does, quick and sideways, so you don't get a good look at his face. "Like it? Think it was funny?"

I had to admit leaving a toilet plunger to his stepfather was fairly hilarious. "That's humor."

"Also there was some serious stuff in there," he said.

"Like thanking Lisa and Janet. I thought that was important because when I die they might not know that I really
like them. Read me yours."

"Nothing to read." I was hungry and that always made
me feel mean.

"Didn't you leave me anything?"

"No." I tore up the paper and stuffed the scraps in my
pocket. "Why aren't they back yet?" I said and I had a
terrible thought. What if Mrs. Francher and her sister
were going to have the food part of the funeral someplace
else, not in their apartment behind the store? I thought
about eating bread and jelly again for lunch and crackers
and pasty milk for supper.

Just then the long black funeral car passed us. It stopped
in front of Francher's Groceteria and Mrs. Francher and
her sister got out. Other cars pulled up, one after the
other. People spilled out, a whole crowd, all of them going
into Mrs. Francher's house.

I spit on my fingers and scrubbed at my cheeks. "Do I
look okay? Is my face clean? You better pull up your pants
so you don't step on them."

"Maybe we shouldn't go, Hanny," Crow said all of a
sudden.

"What? Now you say it? After all this? I know you,
you're getting cold feet just because there's going to be a
bunch of people there. Who cares, Crow? There's going to
be *food.* Don't be gutless."

"If you're so brave, go yourself."

"I will," I shouted, "but you can just forget about eating
any of that food, because I'm not bringing any back for
you, Mr. Crow David Gutless."

"Shut up, Hanny, you have a big fat mouth!"

We went down the street, not speaking. The cars were
gone. The store was locked and dark. In the window a sign
said CLOSED ON ACCOUNT OF A DEATH IN THE FAMILY.
Were they eating up all the food, the meat pies and the
baked ham and the cookies and cakes? I led the way
around the side and knocked on the door.

Nobody came. I knocked again. There was a white lace curtain on the window of the door. "You and your ideas. They're not going to let us in," Crow said, and the door swung open.

"We're here," I said to Mrs. Francher. She was in her stocking feet. She looked at me, then at Crow, as if she expected people, all right, but not us two. "We came to—" I almost said *eat*. I put my hand over my mouth and said, "We came to pay our respects."

"What?"

"Pay our respects." Behind me, I sensed Crow moving away, disappearing down the path.

Mrs. Francher's sister appeared and they stood in the doorway, side by side. They seemed to me like two swollen black balloons. From the room behind them, wonderful smells of meat and cooked fruit drifted toward me. I wanted to cry. "We're here," I said again.

Mrs. Francher looked at her sister. "Oh . . . You take care of it, Celia." She walked away, a funny duck-footed walk in her stocking feet.

"Well . . . well . . ." Mrs. Francher's sister said. "Just you?"

"No, me and my friend. Cr—David," I yelled to him. My mouth was full of saliva and I smiled hard and said, "We were both friends of Mr. Francher's. We were always friends."

Mrs. Francher's sister sighed and looked over her shoulder and finally said, "I suppose you can come in, then."

The living room was warm and crowded. People stood around in little clumps with glasses in their hands, talking. The curtains were drawn and there were pictures and little statues everywhere, on tables, on top of the TV, and on little hanging shelves above the couch.

A long table, loaded with food, took up almost the whole dining room. I squeezed Crow's hand. Our quarrel was forgotten. In the center of the table were two crystal bowls, one filled with apples, pears, grapes, and bananas, the other brimming with a fizzing red punch. There were platters of roast beef, ham, turkey, and salami, little fluted cups filled with butter, a wooden board with a cutting knife, and different kinds of cheeses. There was applesauce and fruit salad, baked potatoes wrapped in silver paper, tomatoes and cucumbers, bread and rolls and cakes and all kinds of hot casseroles.

"What should we do?" Crow whispered.

"Eat," I said, but first I slipped an apple and a pear and slices of ham and roast beef into my pockets. How surprised my mother would be tonight when she came home and found the refrigerator full. "Oh, Hanny," she'd say, "you shouldn't have done that, that's not nice." But she'd eat a slice of roast beef (her favorite) and then polish an apple on her shirt and cut it in half to share with me.

Crow and I filled plates with food. We found a place near a window away from people and began eating as fast as possible. We ate everything on our plates and went back to the table for more. People talked and laughed and no one bothered with us.

Crow's cheeks and lips were shiny with grease. We ate without stopping until neither of us could eat any more.

When we left, I was wonderfully full. Crow rubbed his bulging stomach and whispered, "Well, guess I'll go on living a little longer." And hearing that, I thought without shame how glad I was that Mr. Francher had died and left us this feast. I imagined him looking like a great baby in his coffin, winking at me and saying in his wheezy voice, which had always sounded to me like dark rough honey, "Now, daughter, now, daughter. . . ."

NORMA FOX MAZER

Norma Fox Mazer grew up in Glens Falls, New York, and now lives in the Pompey Hills in central New York with her writer husband, Harry, with whom she wrote *The Solid Gold Kid*. That exciting story of the kidnapping of several teen-agers was named an American Library Association Best Book for Young Adults.

Norma Mazer's novels explore a variety of topics: the effects of divorce on children *(I, Trissy)*, problems of aging *(A Figure of Speech)*, self-image *(Mrs. Fish, Ape, and Me, the Dump Queen)*, and teen-age sexual conflicts *(Up in Seth's Room)*. She has also written about a modern teen-age girl in a prehistoric setting *(Saturday, the Twelfth of October)*, the problems two college students face when they move in together *(Someone to Love)*, and what happens when a divorced father steals his young daughter from her mother *(Taking Terry Mueller)*. That novel won an Edgar Allan Poe Award for Best Juvenile Mystery in 1982.

Critical acclaim has also been bestowed on Mazer's two short-story collections, *Dear Bill, Remember Me? and Other Stories* and *Summer Girls, Love Boys and Other Short Stories*, the first of which was chosen as a *New York Times* Outstanding Book of the Year as well as an ALA Best Book for Young Adults.

Norma Fox Mazer's most recent novel is *When We First Met*, the story of how the love between two teen-agers is affected when the girl discovers that her boyfriend's mother was the driver of the car that accidentally killed her sister a year earlier.

Some rock stars devise elaborate disguises and stay at undisclosed or heavily guarded locations so that they are not disturbed by autograph hunters. But Wendy is a fan who concocts an unusual plan so she can meet her favorite rock musician. . . .

MAY I HAVE YOUR AUTOGRAPH?

MARJORIE SHARMAT

I am sitting in an overstuffed chair in the lobby of The Dominion Imperial International Hotel. So help me, that's really the name. I am surrounded by overgrown ferns, ugly but expensive floral carpeting, chandeliers that make me think of *The Phantom of the Opera,* stuck-up hotel employees in silly-looking uniforms who give me dirty looks—and nobody my age. Except my friend Wendy, who dragged me here.

Wendy is here to meet a guy, but he doesn't know it. In fact, he's never heard of Wendy. But that doesn't stop her from being in love with him. Well, maybe not in love. I think love is for people you've at least met. Wendy has never met Craig the Cat. That's the name of the guy. At least that's his stage name. He's a rock star who's been famous for over six months. Even *my* parents have heard of him.

Wendy is here to get Craig the Cat's autograph on his latest album. On the album jacket, Craig is wearing a black cat costume and he's sitting on a garbage pail with a bottle of spilled milk beside him. He is holding his guitar in his long, furry arms.

Wendy constantly talks about Craig the Cat. But it was like discussing something that was going on in another time frame, on another continent. I didn't mind. It was nicely, safely unreal. Until Craig the Cat came to town today. He's giving a string of benefit performances across the country for some kind of animal group that's devoted to saving "the cats."

"That includes everything from alley cats to exotic tigers," Wendy told me.

"How do you know?"

"I know."

We used our allowance money to buy tickets. That landed us exactly five rows from the back of the auditorium.

"This is so frustrating," Wendy said as we stretched our necks. "I must get closer."

"How close?" I joked.

"I want his autograph," she answered. "I'm not joking."

"Lots of luck."

Wendy doesn't believe in luck. After the concert she dragged me here, to this hotel lobby where we are now sitting. We just sit.

"Are we waiting for him to come into the lobby?" I ask.

"No. He probably got spirited into the hotel through a back or side entrance." Wendy looks at her watch. "He's showered and is relaxing now. He's feeling rested, triumphant, and receptive."

"Receptive to what?"

"To meeting us. To autographing *my* album."

"How are you going to accomplish that? You don't actually know that he's staying at this hotel, and even if he is, you don't know his room number."

Wendy stands up. "Don't be so negative, Rosalind. Come," she says.

I follow her to one of those telephones that connect the caller to hotel rooms. She dials a number. She waits. Then she says, "Craig the Cat, please." She looks at me. "I found him! Listen!" She tilts the receiver so that I, too, can hear what's being said. It's a strain, but I can hear.

A woman is on the other end. "How did you find out

where Craig the Cat is staying?" she asks. "The leak. I need to know where the leak is."

"There isn't any. I'm the only one with the information. Please be nice. I want his autograph."

"Who doesn't."

"Help me get it, please. What are my chances?"

"Poor to nonexistent."

"Oh."

"I'm his manager and, my dear, I'm his mother. I protect Craig from two vantage points. I keep a low profile. Now, how many other fans know where he's staying?"

"None that I know of."

"You mean you didn't peddle the information to the highest bidder?"

"I wouldn't do that."

"Maybe not, dear, but I'm tired of his fans. They tug at Craig's whiskers. They pull his tail. Leave him alone! I'm hanging up."

Click.

Wendy sighs. "We'll just have to wait until he goes into that place over there to eat."

"Haven't you ever heard of room service?"

"Craig doesn't like room service. He doesn't like dining rooms, either. He's a coffee shop person."

"How do you know?"

"I know."

"How did you know his room number?"

"I knew."

"And you knew his mother is his manager?"

"I knew."

We are sitting in the overstuffed chairs again. Wendy is watching and waiting. I see no human-size cat in the lobby. I feel like going to sleep.

Almost an hour goes by. Suddenly, Wendy pokes me. "It's him! It's him!"

I look up. A guy who seems to be about twenty or twenty-five is passing by with a woman who looks old enough to be his mother. He is lean. She is not. They are dressed normally.

I whisper to Wendy. *"That's* Craig the Cat? How do you know? He looks like an ordinary guy."

Wendy doesn't answer. She stands up and starts to follow the guy and the woman. They are heading for the hotel coffee shop. I follow all of them. I see the guy and the woman sit down. They are looking at menus.

Wendy rushes up to them, clutching her album. "May I have your autograph?" she asks the guy.

The woman glares at Wendy. "He doesn't give autographs," she says. "He's just a civilian. Can't you see he's just a civilian?"

"You're Craig the Cat!" Wendy says to the guy.

She says it too loudly.

"How do you know I'm Craig the Cat?" the guy asks. Also too loudly.

People in the coffee shop turn and stare. They repeat, "Craig the Cat!"

Suddenly somebody with a camera materializes and aims the camera at Craig. Wendy bends down and puts her face in front of Craig's. It happens so fast, I can't believe it. The photographer says, "Get out of the way, kid."

Craig's mother glares at the photographer. "Shoo!" she says, waving her hand. "Shoo immediately!"

The photographer leaves. So does Wendy. She runs back to me. I am hiding behind a fern.

Wendy has lost her cool. "Let's get out of here before we're kicked out or arrested," she says.

We rush toward a door.

"Wait!" Someone is yelling at us.

When I hear the word *wait,* it's a signal for me to move even faster. But Wendy stops. "It's *him!"* she says, without turning around.

I turn. It *is* Craig the Cat. He's alone. He rushes up to Wendy. "How did you know me?" he asks. "I didn't tell the media where I was staying. And I certainly didn't give out my room number. I wasn't wearing my cat costume. And I was with my mother. So *how?*"

Wendy looks at me. She's trying to decide if she should answer. Something in her wants to and something in her doesn't want to. She turns back to Craig. "I'm an expert on you," she says. "I know you like fancy, old hotels, and this is the oldest and the fanciest in town. I know your lucky number is twelve, so I figured you'd stay on the twelfth floor in room 1212. I know you always wear red socks when you're not performing. So tonight I watched ankles in the lobby. And I knew you'd be with your manager—your mother."

"What about the photographer?"

"I know you don't want to be photographed without your cat costume. In an interview of October eighth of this year, you said it would wreck your feline image. So when I saw the photographer trying to take your picture, I put my face in front of yours."

"You did that for me?"

"I'd do it for any special friend."

"But you don't know me."

"Yes, I do. When I read about someone, I get to know him. I don't believe everything I read, of course. I pick out certain parts. I look for the reality behind the unreality. I went through seventy-one pages about Craig the Cat, in eleven different magazines, and I ended up thinking of you as my friend."

Craig the Cat is staring at Wendy as if *he's* the fan. He's in awe of *her!* It's nothing very earthshaking. It's not like there's a crowd roaring or it's a summit meeting of world leaders or a momentous change in the universe. It's just a small, nice moment in the lobby of The Dominion Imperial International Hotel, and it will never go away for Wendy.

We're back in the hotel coffee shop. Four of us are sitting around a table, eating. Craig's mother is beaming benevolently like a contented mother cat presiding over her brood, which now includes Wendy and me in addition to Craig. After we finish eating, Wendy hands her record album to Craig. "Now may I have your autograph?" she asks.

Craig pulls out a pen and writes on the album jacket. I hope that Wendy will show me what he writes. Maybe she won't. Whatever she does will be okay, though. Maybe this will be the first private entry in her collection of reality and unreality about her new friend, Craig the Cat. She's entitled.

As for me, I'm now sitting in a chair in a hotel coffee shop as a new and honored member of this Clan of the Cat. It has been a strange and kind of wonderful day, thanks to my friend, Wendy the Expert. I'm glad I'm here. If you take away some of the ferns and a few fat chairs and most of the carpeting, The Dominion Imperial International Hotel definitely has possibilities.

MARJORIE SHARMAT

At the age of eight, Marjorie Weinman Sharmat published *The Snooper's Gazette* with a friend in Portland, Maine. She is now best known to younger readers for her more than sixty books for children, including the popular *Nate the Great* and the *Maggie Marmelstein* books, several of which have been Junior Literary Guild selections.

Marjorie Sharmat entered the young adult field in 1982 by writing the novelization of the hilarious CBS-TV situation comedy *Square Pegs*. She followed that with her own first novel for teens, *I Saw Him First*. Her most recent young adult books are *How to Meet a Gorgeous Guy* and *How to Meet a Gorgeous Girl*.

Mrs. Sharmat lives in Tucson, Arizona, with her husband Mitchell (who is also an author of books for children), their son Andrew, and their dog Fritz Melvin. Miss America, their old pet chicken, Marjorie Sharmat says, has "gone to that great barnyard in the sky."

"May I Have Your Autograph?" was inspired by her son Craig, a professional guitarist performing in Las Vegas.

Everyone has heard tales about alligators living in the sewers beneath the streets of New York City. Similar strange tales are also told about that city's subway tunnels. Unlike those stories of horrifying experiences, this next story reveals a beautiful, though sad, secret about other residents of the subway tunnels. . . .

MIDNIGHT SNACK

DIANE DUANE

Dad came down with the flu that week, so I had to go down to the subway and feed the unicorns. That was okay, but Jerry saw me going down the street Thursday night and started following me. Now normally *that* would be okay too—even if he does call me "Frogface" all the time. But that night the timing was lousy.

"Where ya goin', Froggy?" he shouted, even though it was perfectly obvious—I was taking the usual shortcut across the pizza place's parking lot, to the Shop-Rite. What he wasn't going to understand was why I wasn't going *into* the supermarket, but around back. They throw pretty fair stuff out there, the beat-up vegetables and bread and such that not even the charity groups want. You can pick up quite a bit if you get there before the bag-ladies do.

I didn't answer Jerry back, so when I went around to the dumpsters, naturally he came after me. He sounded a little worried. "Froggo? Whatcha doin'?"

"Go play in traffic, Friedman," I said. I was annoyed. This wasn't something he should be seeing, but I didn't have the time to waste on chasing him away—the unicorns don't wait around long. I got a paper bag from inside my jacket and started going through the first dumpster. Jerry looked at me as if I was from Mars.

"You okay?"

"Yeah, fine." I found half a squashed head of lettuce and some prune Danish that were just a little moldy around the edges.

"Your dad get fired or something?" He really sounded worried about me now. This was real cute coming from the kid who once took the locking washers off the wheels of my skateboard as a surprise.

"I'm fine, *bug off!*" I felt stupid then, for shouting so loud the whole city could have heard. The only thing I could think of to do was turn around and shove the squashed lettuce into his hands.

He stared at it. "But what—?"

"I'm going to feed the unicorns," I said, hoping he'd think I was nuts and go away. Sure enough, he looked up from the lettuce with an expression that would make you hide your skateboard.

"You've finally flipped out. . . ."

"Right," I said. "Come on, you can call the men in the white coats after I'm done." I threw the butt end of a bunch of celery into the brown bag, got down from the dumpster, and headed off fast.

He didn't even begin catching up with me till halfway down the stairs to the Lexington Avenue Local station. It looked the way it usually looks that time of night—dingy concrete, dull light bulbs, peeling theater posters and cigarette ads. I was through the turnstile and a good way down the platform when he hollered after me again. He sounded upset this time. "Frog?"

I turned. He was on the other side of the turnstile with the lettuce in his hands, and the black lady in the change booth was staring at him. "I don't have a token," he said.

"Wha'd you say? 'Frog'?" I stuck a finger in one ear and started cleaning it.

"Oh, all right. *Beth*—"

I pitched him a token and headed down the platform

again. In a few seconds he caught up with me. "What're we doing, *really?*" he said, whispering loudly.

"I told you."

"Oh, give me a *break!*"

"Shut up, smogbrain, you'll scare them!" There was no one else on the platform—I looked up and down it, checking to see that no one was hiding in the tunnel either. The rails ticked a little as an express train squealed in on the lower level.

"Scare *who?*"

I leaned back against the wall at the very end of the platform, because it was a long story, or it had been when Dad told it to me. And I told Jerry the whole thing—what we thought was true, anyway. How the city had grown around the unicorns, hemming them in. Some of them couldn't adapt, Dad said, and so they stayed in the deep places in Central Park and never came out. But some of them were bolder—or not as smart. They'd learned to hide in the subway tunnels, always moving, hiding from the trains and the people. The bravest of the downstairs unicorns sneak up onto the street sometimes, on moonless nights or cloudy ones, or during power failures. They're the reason the grass around trees on city streets never grows long. But most of them aren't so brave. The shy ones stay in the tunnels all the time. And because of the litter laws, people don't throw so much food on the tracks for them to pick up anymore. The shy ones starve, sometimes. And the shy ones are the prettiest. . . .

Jerry listened to all this with the hide-your-skateboard look on his face. But he didn't say anything till I ran out of words and started to blush—there's something special about those shy ones, something about their eyes; I felt dumb talking to a boy about it. Maybe Jerry saw me getting red. At least when he spoke up, he didn't sound like he was teasing. "How do you know so much about this? Why hasn't someone else seen them before?"

"They have." I still remembered that night Dad came home late from work, looking pale. He hardly said anything at dinner, and after everybody went to bed, I could hear him and Mom talking through the walls—not the words, but their voices. Dad sounded unhappy at first, then upset; and Mom got loud and finally told him to go to sleep, he'd been drinking too much again. *That* I heard clearly. For a couple of days he looked awful and kept muttering all the time—he does that when things are bugging him. Finally he waited till Mom was out food shopping, and sat me down in the living room. I was scared to death; I thought he was going to tell me about the facts of life. Instead he told me about the unicorn he'd seen run out of the tunnel at Fulton Street. It had come out just long enough to grab up a stale half-bagel smeared with cracked cream cheese, someone's garbage thrown out on the tracks, and run back again. He cried when he told me. I nearly died. I'd never seen him cry about anything; it looked impossible. His face got all bent. "The poor creature," he kept mumbling while he cried: "Poor little thing!" The next day we got some day-old bread and let my mother think we were going to Central Park to feed the ducks. But the ducks went without. They're fat enough.

I didn't tell Jerry about my Dad, though. "Some of the subway people who work down here—they've seen them. They leave them food in places where the rats won't get it. And they don't tell. If they told, there'd be all sorts of stuff happening. TV news people, with cameras and bright lights. Scientists. The Board of Health, for all I know. And the unicorns would go in deep, under the streets, and never come out again, and they'd all starve." I looked at Jerry. His face was so blank it made me scared. "So keep your mouth shut!"

"I better," he said, real quietly, looking past me. "They're here."

I turned around. The eyes had caught him as they'd caught me that first time. You might think they were cats' eyes, except cats always have that kind of strangeness about them, when their eyes flash at you in the headlights.

If humans' eyes flashed in the dark, they would look like this. Only the shape is wrong—the eyes are spaced wide like a horse's. The pair of glimmers looked at us from the dark. Looked mostly at Jerry, rather; they knew my voice by now. One pair of eyes, then two, a dull pink reflection in the tired subway lighting—just hanging out there where the track vanished into shadow.

They had no names. Dad and I always thought of names on the way to the subway, or on the way back; but seeing the unicorns, the names seemed cheap—they fell off. I felt around in the bag for the celery. Green stuff was always good to start with—they got so little of it, the shy ones. One of them heard the crunch of the celery snapping and took a step forward, barely into the light.

I heard Jerry's breath go in as if someone had punched him. It was the same for him as it'd been for me the first time. Nothing that lives in a subway should be that graceful. Cats run, rats and mice scurry. But the unicorns just flow out of the darkness, and not even the cinders crunch when they put their feet down. Sometimes, if they're playful, they walk on the rails like somebody on a tightrope, and don't slip or make a sound. This one just took one step and stretched his neck out like a swan on the lake when it doesn't want to come too close. The unicorn's horn glinted, pearly, the only bright thing about him—everywhere else he was the iron-rust color of the gravel between the tracks. His eyes were so brown they were black. But the end of his horn caught the light like the edge of a knife as he stepped out. "Hey, they sharpen them back there," Dad had said one night, when a touch of a horn drew blood from his hand. Maybe they fought among themselves; or maybe there were things down there that tried to eat them. I didn't want to think about it.

"Give him some," I whispered at Jerry, annoyed again; he was making them wait. "Throw it. They won't eat out of your hand." Jerry tore off some lettuce and threw it down on the tracks. The brown one looked at him for a moment, then put its head down to eat. You could see it was starving; every rib showed. But it lowered its head slow as a king sipping wine.

More came while the first was eating. Maybe he was the herd leader and had been checking the place out. Whatever, the tracks were full in a few moments—nothing but tails switching and necks stretching and eyes, those eyes. All the unicorns were dark this time, though I'd seen ones with white socks or blazes, and once a tan one with a light mane like a palomino's. These weren't any fatter than any others I'd seen, though, and while they ate gracefully, they did it fast. Two of them, a rusty one and a black, got rowdy and waved their horns at each other over a piece of the Danish. Jerry threw them more, and they stopped and each gobbled a piece.

They were close, right up by the platform. I'd never seen them so close. Jerry was so amazed by the whole thing, and the rusty one standing right in front of him with its lower jaw going around and around—even unicorns look a little funny when they chew—that he nearly lost his balance and fell down when the black unicorn snuck up beside him and grabbed at the rest of the Danish in his hand. Even though he was surprised, though, Jerry didn't let go for a second. He just stood there looking at the black, while it tugged at the Danish and gazed back at him with those deep, sad eyes. I know that look. My eyes started burning, and my nose filled up. Nothing that lives in a subway should be that proud, and that hungry, and feel that helpless. Nothing that lives *anywhere* should. The black unicorn got the last piece of Danish away from Jerry and ate it, delicately, but fast. Jerry looked a moment at the hand the unicorn had touched, and then wiped his nose on the sleeve of his jacket.

All their heads went up then, all at once, as if they were a herd of gazelles in a nature movie when the lion's coming. They stared down the tracks toward the downtown end—and there was just a flicker of motion, and they were gone, headed uptown and into the dark too fast to really see. Jerry looked over at me and opened his mouth—then shut it again as he started to hear what they'd heard: the ticking and the rumbling and the squeal of metal a long way down at the next station. I crumpled up the bag and stuck it inside my jacket. We waited for the train to come in—it would've looked weird to just go down to the platform and then come up again before a train came. The subway seemed much louder than usual, especially compared to the quiet ones who'd been on the tracks a few moments before.

Fifteen or twenty people got off, and we went up the stairs with them. Jerry wiped his nose again, and sniffed. "Subway people feed them?"

"And my Dad."

"I thought they only came to virgins."

So had my Dad. "I dunno," I said. "Maybe they can't afford to be so picky anymore." That was one thing Dad had said. I didn't tell Jerry the other, what Dad had said the first time one let him touch it—him, a man who empties garbage cans for a living, and comes home smelling like what the city throws away. He'd looked at his hands like Jerry had, and finally he said, "It must be love." And he'd sat down and watched baseball that whole night and said not another word.

"You feed them every night?" Jerry said.

"When we can. Sometimes it's every other night. My mom gets suspicious and thinks Dad's out messing around, or I'm sneaking off doing drugs or something."

We got up to the street. Jerry snorted at the thought. "*You* do *drugs?* You wouldn't know which side of your nose to put the marijuana up."

That was true, so I punched him a good one in the arm and he yelped. When we were about halfway to my building, Jerry said all of a sudden, "What about survival of the fittest, though? Maybe only the strong ones should live, to make more strong ones. . . ."

I thought about that for a moment. "Well, yeah. Normally. But this isn't normal. They were here first. Then we built all this around them." I waved my arms at the city in general. "Maybe there's nothing wrong with helping them handle it. They're an endangered species."

Jerry nodded and wiped his nose again. "Survival *with* the fittest," he said.

He was smart. That was one of the reasons I didn't mind him following me sometimes. Maybe even *this* time had been a good idea. "Yeah," I said.

"You gonna feed them tomorrow?"

"I think so. Dad's still sick."

"Can I come with you?"

I looked at him. "If you go to the A&P first. I'll go to the Shop-Rite, and meet you. We'll have twice as much."

"Great." He looked down the street at my building. "Race you?"

"Okay."

"Go!"

After about half a minute he tripped me. I'm used to always having my elbows and knees skinned, but I don't think Jerry's real used to having black eyes. He was going to have some explaining to do at school the next day.

As long as it didn't make him late for feeding time, though, neither of us cared.

DIANE DUANE

Ten years ago, Diane Duane gave up a career as a psychiatric nurse to devote herself to a career she had been pursuing since she was eight: writing science fiction and fantasy. She has since been twice nominated for the John W. Campbell Award for best new science fiction writer of the year.

In the past five years she has written extensively for Saturday morning television. Her recent publications include the new "Star Trek" novel *The Wounded Sky,* the young adult fantasy *So You Want to Be a Wizard,* and the second volume of the "Middle Kingdoms" high-fantasy tetralogy, *The Door into Shadow.*

A sixth-generation New Yorker, she lives alternately on the East and West coasts with her cat, Yoda, and her half-Arab palomino gelding, Harlie.

"Midnight Snack" has been adapted as a half-hour animated TV special, in cooperation with WQED in Pittsburgh.

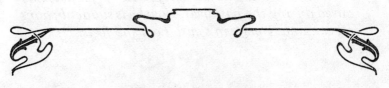

TURMOILS

Tracy hadn't seen her father very much since he moved out. She had hated him for all the pain he had caused during the past year. Now he is suddenly gone forever, and Tracy isn't sure how she feels. . . .

PIGEON HUMOR

SUSAN BETH PFEFFER

The May sun beat down on the black limousine, and Tracy winced as her bare legs touched the car seat. Her mother had told her to wear stockings, but she'd refused, knowing there'd be a scene that morning over it, which there was. It was childish, she knew, but she was feeling childish. And why shouldn't she? When better to feel childish than on the day of your father's funeral.

"There's room for all of us," her uncle Barry announced as he squeezed in next to Tracy's mother. "Come on, Sheila, there's plenty of room."

"All right," Sheila said. "There is room, isn't there?"

"Yes, it's a lovely limo," Tracy's mother said.

"My first limo ride," Tracy said.

"May it be the first of many," Barry said. "Only I hope on happier occasions."

"Yes, certainly," Sheila said. She reached over her husband and her sister to pat Tracy's hand.

It was funny, Tracy thought, the only one of them in black was the chauffeur. The rest of them were wearing dark dignified colors, but no black, except for Sheila's purse and shoes. Even her mother's accessories were navy blue. Maybe the chauffeur was the only one in mourning. Maybe he was the only one who really cared.

"Are you all right?" Sheila asked. "How are you holding up, Tracy?"

"I'm fine," she replied. "Really."

"I remember when my father died," Barry said. "Of course, I was a lot older than Tracy is."

"I don't think we really want to hear about it right now, dear," Sheila said.

"No, that's okay," Tracy said. Anything would be better than silence. Her mother hadn't been talking to her since the stocking debate that morning.

"No," Barry replied. "Sheila's probably right. It's just I know how devastating it can be when your father dies."

Was that what this was? Tracy wondered. Was she devastated? She knew she was something, had been since the phone call three days before. She had the vaguest feeling that even as the phone rang she knew it was bad news, but of course that was hindsight. Still, she'd known something was terribly wrong when she recognized the voice on the other end. It was Cherry, her father's girl friend, asking to speak to her mother. Cherry and her mother didn't speak. Only disaster could have made Cherry call.

"He's dead," her mother told her after a conversation of "umphs" and "yes I sees." "He died at Cherry's apartment an hour ago. Just like him to die in the apartment of someone named Cherry."

He'd been living with Cherry for almost a year, waiting for the divorce to be finalized before marrying her. But he wasn't supposed to die. There was no reason for him to die.

"His heart went out on him," her mother declared. "What do you expect, taking up with a little chickie. It'd kill any man."

"He's dead?" Tracy asked. Maybe she'd misunderstood, maybe he'd had a heart attack. Older men were always having those, especially in the beds of their younger girl friends.

"Dead as a doorknob," her mother replied. "Cherry called for an ambulance, but it was all over before they even got there. Sorry, honey."

"Yeah," Tracy said. Dead. She'd wished him dead often

enough in the past year, a year where she'd seen him only
four times. Three times at Cherry's, with her hovering
over the two of them, repeatedly asking Tracy if she'd like
something to eat or drink, a Coke maybe, or some after-
dinner mints. They hadn't even had dinner and Cherry
was pushing after-dinner mints on her. Four times and
three of them with after-dinner mints. Just once she and
her father had been alone, so they could talk, try to reach
an understanding of what had happened, what it was going to do to the two of them. And that had been a disaster,
them sitting in the middle of the park, with Tracy crying,
and then her father crying, until the autumn chill forced
them up and back to their respective homes. That was the
last time she'd been alone with him, and all she could
remember was how foolish he had looked, his eyes puffy
from crying, no way to wipe his nose, since he had given
his handkerchief to Tracy.

"It was a nice service," Sheila said, after it was all finished. Tracy sensed everyone's relief that the funeral had
ended without disaster.

"Yes," Barry said. "Very nice. Very moving."

Tracy's mother snorted. "It moved my stomach, made
me want to throw up."

"Really, Phyllis," Sheila said, and gestured slightly with
her head toward Tracy. "It was very tasteful."

Tracy's mother snorted again, but she didn't say anything. It was nice having her silent, Tracy decided. Better
than it had been for three days, with her mother cursing
her father's death. Tracy thought her mother would prefer to be a widow than a divorcee, but it didn't seem to
stop the flow of curses. He was bound not to have left
them anything. He was bound to have let the insurance
lapse. He was bound to have figured out a way to deprive
them of his pension, of his social security, of his bank
account, assuming he had any money left in it, which was
unlikely, given Cherry's expensive tastes. There was sure
to be no estate, and if there was an estate, they'd be
cheated out of it. And she'd be stuck with the funeral

expenses, probate, all the mess that death entails. Tracy should expect no economic miracles from this death. No trust funds, no money for her college education, nothing good, nothing good at all.

Tracy had long since given up expecting anything from her parents beyond food, shelter, and arguments. The arguments had been halved when her father moved out, and they might disappear altogether now. That would be inheritance enough.

"I heard a cute joke the other day," Barry said, trying to fill the silence. "Really cute."

Tracy sighed. Barry had two schools of jokes: cute and good. Cute he'd tell in front of her and his children. Good were dirty, and when she was lucky he'd tell them in front of her, forgetting she was still a kid. But it was too much to hope for that he'd be telling a dirty joke in the limo after her father's funeral.

"What is it, dear?" Sheila asked. "I'm sure we could all use a good laugh right now."

"It's kind of long," Barry said. "I'll try to give you the abridged version."

"That's okay," Tracy's mother declared. "We're not going anywhere."

"No, no," Barry said. "It'll still be funny if it's short. You see, there are these two birds. Pigeons. Leonard and Cora."

"I love pigeon jokes," Sheila said.

"Anyway, Leonard lives in Philadelphia and Cora lives in New York," Barry said. "They met in Atlantic City and it was love at first sight. Only neither one of them wanted to give up their homes, move to the other one's city. They had family where they were, loved their individual homes. And it was still early in their relationship, so they decided they'd see each other on weekends. One weekend Leonard would fly down to New York, next weekend Cora would fly up to Philadelphia."

"The other way around," Tracy's mother said. "Philadelphia is south of New York."

"Up, down, you know what I mean," Barry said impatiently. "Anyway it was Leonard's turn to fly down, I mean up, to New York. He was scheduled to arrive on Friday evening, spend the whole weekend with Cora, only it got to be seven, eight o'clock and there's no Leonard. Naturally, Cora's frantic. Where can he be? Was there some sort of terrible accident? Was he jilting her? Was there another pigeon in his life?"

"Oh, dear," Sheila said. "I know how nerve-racking that can be."

"Finally at ten o'clock, in comes Leonard. By this time Cora's hysterical. 'Where were you?' she screeches at Leonard. 'Do you know what time it is?' "

" 'I'm sorry dear,' Leonard says. 'It was just such a nice evening I decided to walk.' "

Barry waited for the others to laugh. Sheila did, and Tracy's mother grunted reluctantly. Tracy smiled. It was a cute joke, she supposed. But she didn't seem to be in the mood for pigeon humor just then.

"You know, honey, you don't have to come back with us," Sheila told Tracy as the limo drove them back to the funeral home. "I know that was the plan, but if you've changed your mind, really it's all right."

"No, that's okay," Tracy said. "I'd like to go to your house for the weekend. If it wouldn't bother you too much."

"You're never a bother," Sheila replied, and she gave Tracy a hug. Tracy held on for a second longer than normal. A second longer than that and she might never have broken away. For a brief agonizing moment she envied Sheila's two daughters their parents, their home, their lives. But then the feeling passed. It was enough to have Barry and Sheila to visit, to hug, to count on every once in a while. Like now. Whether they wanted her or not, she was theirs for the weekend. She couldn't stay a minute longer with her mother, and she doubted her mother could stay a minute longer with her.

"It's just we have to go to the band recital tonight,"

Sheila said apologetically. "It means so much to Rachel for us to be there."

Rachel was eleven, and when she was disappointed about something, no one in the state was safe.

"It's okay," Tracy said. "It's fine, really."

"Jessica's at a sleepaway tonight," Sheila said. "So she won't be pestering you. You can have her room."

"Great," Tracy answered. She could sleep with all Jessica's teddy bears on the bed. It was a canopied bed, too. Between the canopy and the teddy bears she'd be hidden from sight forever.

"You don't have to go to the band recital," Barry said. "You know that, Tracy. You can stay home and watch TV if you prefer."

"Oh, dear, I don't know," Sheila said. "Do you really think it's a good idea for Tracy to be alone tonight?"

"*I'm* going to be alone tonight," Tracy's mother declared. "Not that anybody seems to care about that."

"Of course we care, Phyllis," Sheila said. "And if this band recital weren't so important to Rachel, I'd spend the night at your house. You know how Rachel is."

"Oh, certainly," Tracy's mother replied. "I understand how her band recital counts a lot more than me. It's certainly more important than my husband's death."

"Oh, come on now, Phyllis," Barry said.

"I'll stay home if you want, Mom," Tracy said.

"No, that's all right," her mother replied. "Go, stay with your aunt and uncle. Enjoy yourself. You deserve a good time after all this."

"I don't know how good a time she'll have at an elementary school band recital," Barry said. "It's not my idea of fine art."

"It's bound to be more entertaining than I am," Tracy's mother said. No one disputed this.

"We're all tired," Sheila said. "But now that the funeral is over, things are bound to improve."

"I'll get my stuff out of the car," Tracy offered as the limo pulled into the parking lot. She was glad for the reason to break away. She got her overnight bag out of the trunk of her mother's car, and walked over to Barry and Sheila's station wagon, waiting for them to join her. She watched them exchanging farewells with her mother, the awkward hugs and kisses, and then their slightly too eager steps toward their car. Barry unlocked the doors, and Tracy got in the backseat. There were remnants of Rachel and Jessica there, a hair ribbon, a candy wrapper, a tiny comb with doll's hair stuck in its teeth. Tracy listened to the comforting drone from the front seat, murmured the appropriate noises when she had to, but otherwise kept silent. Silent felt good. She hadn't thought a funeral could be so noisy.

The quiet continued through the rest of the afternoon. She hid in Jessica's room, pretending to sleep, thinking about nothing, everything, the school she'd missed, the test in biology, the assembly that morning with a guest speaker on drug abuse. She thought about flowers and summer vacations and how much noise could hurt. She thought about teddy bears and canopied beds and little girls lucky enough to have both. There were also a couple of moments, dazzling in their pain, when she thought about her father and how he no longer existed.

"It's really very nice of you to come," Sheila whispered to Tracy that evening as they took their seats in the elementary school assembly hall. "You can't imagine how much it means to Rachel to know you're here. She looks up to you so much."

"It's okay," Tracy said. "I like Rachel. This should be fun."

"It's more likely to be murder," Barry said. "All the kids slaughtering great music."

"Really," Sheila said disapprovingly. "The important thing is it gives the children a real appreciation of music. Rachel is obviously never going to be a professional violinist, but it's so good for her to have these lessons. And a chance to show off."

"I like bad music," Tracy said cheerfully.

"Then you're definitely in the right place," Barry said. "Shush, both of you," Sheila said. "Maybe the kids will fool us. Rachel's certainly been rehearsing enough."

"Oh, no," Barry moaned, as the curtain rose, revealing a large number of wriggling school-age musicians. "We who are about to die . . ."

"Barry!" Sheila said, a little louder than she should have. The people sitting around them gave her disapproving looks. Tracy, seeing her aunt blushing slightly, smiled to herself.

The first piece the orchestra played was a march by John Philip Sousa. It was loud and busy, with an incessant thumping beat. Migraine music, Tracy's mother would have called it, but Tracy liked it well enough.

The second number, unfortunately, was something else again. It favored violins, and an entire chorus of off-tune kids. It took a few moments for Tracy to realize what song they were mangling, and then it came to her. "Yesterday."

It wasn't a song with any great emotional significance in her life. Just one she'd heard over and over again, on the radio, in supermarkets, once in an elevator. She remembered how startled she had been to learn that even they were wired for Muzak. But she'd never heard it performed so resoundingly badly before. Slurred words, singers losing track of lyrics, violins piercing the air with horrible scratching noises. So much noise. Loud, happy, excited, terrible terrible noise.

In spite of herself, Tracy realized she was laughing. The band was so bad they were funny. It was all so funny. Her laughter continued, growing sharper and more frantic, until she found herself crying from the laughter, tears pouring out of her eyes, down her cheeks, rivers of tears, all from the bad music. The laughter turned to silent heaves, but the tears couldn't be stopped, couldn't be hidden.

"Tracy, are you all right?" Sheila asked. "Tracy, what is it?"

For a moment all Tracy could see was confusion, and then it came to her. She couldn't tell Sheila that it was Rachel's band, that it was Rachel who had done this to her.

"The joke," she managed to gasp, between the laughter and the sobs.

"What?" Sheila asked.

"The joke," Tracy said. "The joke about pigeons. 'Such a nice day, I decided to walk.' " She had never laughed so hard in her life. The band continued playing, the chorus kept on its efforts at singing. Thank God for Barry and his dumb joke. " 'Such a nice day,' " she repeated, hoping Sheila would believe her, hoping it was all right to be laughing at the joke during Rachel's recital, hoping when the band stopped playing she'd be able to stop laughing, hoping people didn't really die laughing, hoping the pain now started would someday stop, hoping, just hoping and laughing and crying and hoping.

SUSAN BETH PFEFFER

Born in New York City and a graduate of New York University, Susan Beth Pfeffer lives in Middletown, New York. She is a free-lance writer of reviews, articles, and juvenile books, including *Better Than All Right, Just Between Us,* and *What Do You Do When Your Mouth Won't Open?*

Ms. Pfeffer attracted the attention of teen-age readers first with *Marly the Kid* and then with *The Beauty Queen* and *Starring Peter and Leigh. Marly the Kid* is the story of a teen-ager who runs away from her mother to live with her father and understanding stepmother and then gets into trouble in school by challenging her sexist teacher.

Defying school authorities is also an issue in *A Matter of Principle,* where the principal censors the student newspaper and then expels a group of students when they publish an underground newspaper.

About David concerns the suicide of a teen-age boy and the reactions of his closest friend. The American Library Association selected *About David* as a Best Book for Young Adults.

Susan Beth Pfeffer's most recent book is *Courage, Dana!*

Almost every school has a bully who roams the halls picking on smaller, weaker kids. Such individuals are tough, mean, insensitive. No one is safe from their assaults. It seems as if there is no way to stop them, no way to get back at them. Isn't there anything that anybody can do? . . .

PRISCILLA AND THE WIMPS

RICHARD PECK

Listen, there was a time when you couldn't even go to the *rest room* around this school without a pass. And I'm not talking about those little pink tickets made out by some teacher. I'm talking about a pass that could cost anywhere up to a buck, sold by Monk Klutter.

Not that Mighty Monk ever touched money, not in public. The gang he ran, which ran the school for him, was his collection agency. They were Klutter's Kobras, a name spelled out in nailheads on six well-known black plastic windbreakers.

Monk's threads were more . . . subtle. A pile-lined suede battle jacket with lizard-skin flaps over tailored Levis and a pair of ostrich-skin boots, brassed-toed and suitable for kicking people around. One of his Kobras did nothing all day but walk a half step behind Monk, carrying a fitted bag with Monk's gym shoes, a roll of rest-room passes, a cashbox, and a switchblade that Monk gave himself manicures with at lunch over at the Kobras' table.

Speaking of lunch, there were a few cases of advanced malnutrition among the newer kids. The ones who were a little slow in handing over a cut of their lunch money and were therefore barred from the cafeteria. Monk ran a tight ship.

I admit it. I'm five foot five, and when the Kobras slithered by, with or without Monk, I shrank. And I admit this, too: I paid up on a regular basis. And I might add: so would you.

This school was old Monk's Garden of Eden. Unfortunately for him, there was a serpent in it. The reason Monk didn't recognize trouble when it was staring him in the face is that the serpent in the Kobras' Eden was a girl.

Practically every guy in school could show you his scars. Fang marks from Kobras, you might say. And they were all highly visible in the shower room: lumps, lacerations, blue bruises, you name it. But girls usually got off with a warning.

Except there was this one girl named Priscilla Roseberry. Picture a girl named Priscilla Roseberry, and you'll be light years off. Priscilla was, hands down, the largest student in our particular institution of learning. I'm not talking fat. I'm talking big. Even beautiful, in a bionic way. Priscilla wasn't inclined toward organized crime. Otherwise, she could have put together a gang that would turn Klutter's Kobras into garter snakes.

Priscilla was basically a loner except she had one friend. A little guy named Melvin Detweiler. You talk about The Odd Couple. Melvin's one of the smallest guys above midget status ever seen. A really nice guy, but, you know —little. They even had lockers next to each other, in the same bank as mine. I don't know what they had going. I'm not saying this was a romance. After all, people deserve their privacy.

Priscilla was sort of above everything, if you'll pardon a pun. And very calm, as only the very big can be. If there was anybody who didn't notice Klutter's Kobras, it was Priscilla.

Until one winter day after school when we were all grabbing our coats out of our lockers. And hurrying, since Klutter's Kobras made sweeps of the halls for after-school shakedowns.

Anyway, up to Melvin's locker swaggers one of the

Kobras. Never mind his name. Gang members don't need names. They've got group identity. He reaches down and grabs little Melvin by the neck and slams his head against his locker door. The sound of skull against steel rippled all the way down the locker row, speeding the crowds on their way.

"Okay, let's see your pass," snarls the Kobra.

"A pass for what this time?" Melvin asks, probably still dazed.

"Let's call it a pass for very short people," says the Kobra, "a dwarf tax." He wheezes a little Kobra chuckle at his own wittiness. And already he's reaching for Melvin's wallet with the hand that isn't circling Melvin's windpipe. All this time, of course, Melvin and the Kobra are standing in Priscilla's big shadow.

She's taking her time shoving her books into her locker and pulling on a very large-size coat. Then, quicker than the eye, she brings the side of her enormous hand down in a chop that breaks the Kobra's hold on Melvin's throat. You could hear a pin drop in that hallway. Nobody'd ever laid a finger on a Kobra, let alone a hand the size of Priscilla's.

Then Priscilla, who hardly ever says anything to anybody except to Melvin, says to the Kobra, "Who's your leader, wimp?"

This practically blows the Kobra away. First he's chopped by a girl, and now she's acting like she doesn't know Monk Klutter, the Head Honcho of the World. He's so amazed, he tells her. "Monk Klutter."

"Never heard of him," Priscilla mentions. "Send him to see me." The Kobra just backs away from her like the whole situation is too big for him, which it is.

Pretty soon Monk himself slides up. He jerks his head once, and his Kobras slither off down the hall. He's going to handle this interesting case personally. "Who is it around here doesn't know Monk Klutter?"

He's standing inches from Priscilla, but since he'd have

to look up at her, he doesn't. "Never heard of him," says Priscilla.

Monk's not happy with this answer, but by now he's spotted Melvin, who's grown smaller in spite of himself. Monk breaks his own rule by reaching for Melvin with his own hands. "Kid," he says, "you're going to have to educate your girl friend."

His hands never quite make it to Melvin. In a move of pure poetry Priscilla has Monk in a hammerlock. His neck's popping like gunfire, and his head's bowed under the immense weight of her forearm. His suede jacket's peeling back, showing pile.

Priscilla's behind him in another easy motion. And with a single mighty thrust forward, frog-marches Monk into her own locker. It's incredible. His ostrich-skin boots click once in the air. And suddenly he's gone, neatly wedged into the locker, a perfect fit. Priscilla bangs the door shut, twirls the lock, and strolls out of school. Melvin goes with her, of course, trotting along below her shoulder. The last stragglers leave quietly.

Well, this is where fate, an even bigger force than Priscilla, steps in. It snows all that night, a blizzard. The whole town ices up. And school closes for a week.

RICHARD PECK

Richard Peck, a former English teacher who was born in Decatur, Illinois, has published a number of novels, several poems, a collection of essays, and three poetry anthologies for teen-agers: *Sounds and Silences, Pictures That Storm Inside My Head,* and *Mindscapes.*

Among his earliest novels are *Dreamland Lake, Don't Look and It Won't Hurt, Through a Brief Darkness,* and *Representing Superdoll. Are You in the House Alone?,* a first-person account of the rape of a teen-ager and its subsequent effects, and *Father Figure,* the story of a teen-ager's relationship with the father who abandoned him and then returns after the death of the boy's mother, were both made-for-TV movies that have attracted an adult as well as a teen-age audience. Both of those novels, as well as several of his other books, were chosen as Best Books for Young Adults by the American Library Association. One of his most recent novels is a romance told by a boy, entitled *Close Enough to Touch.*

Younger readers have enjoyed Peck's series of ghost stories, starting with *The Ghost Belonged to Me,* followed by *Ghosts I Have Been.* Blossom Culp, the self-assured narrator of the second book, is featured again in his newest novel, *The Dreadful Future of Blossom Culp.*

People who enjoy visiting shopping malls and think someone could live forever inside one can consider the details of such an existence in *Secrets of the Shopping Mall,* where several kids *do* live totally inside a mall. Mr. Peck, however, lives alternately in New York City and New Milford, Connecticut. He is also the author of three novels for adults, most recently *This Family of Women.*

Sometimes, deep inside, we know we have a special problem. But on the surface we fail to recognize or accept it. We gloss over it, cover it up, deny its existence. Until something happens that brings it all, suddenly and surprisingly, to the surface. . . .

WELCOME

OUIDA SEBESTYEN

My father's Aunt Dessie peered through the windshield at a road sign. "Slow up a little bit, Mary," she told my mother. "The last time I tried to find kinfolks I hadn't visited for a while, I got the house number and the street perfect, but I was in the wrong town." She turned to me in the back seat. "I ran across this yard yelling, 'Guess who's here, Annabelle,' and burst right in on a white lady. Perfect stranger."

I caught my mother's eyes in the rearview mirror and made a pretend smile for Aunt Dessie, thinking how I would describe her to my friend Sharon when I got home. *Picture this eighty-year-old drill sergeant? In drag? With this head of corn-row hair she must have made with a real hoe?* Sharon would double up. At least as far as she could double, now.

My mother slowed to a creep. Yesterday evening, bowling along through Texas on her way to see her parents, she had swerved off the interstate toward a dismal little town. Before I could figure what in blazes she was doing, we were spending the night on Aunt Dessie's let-down couch between two whatnots crammed with spinster junk. I had hissed, "What *is* this—I hate changes." But my mother just lay with her back to me, pretending to be asleep, while strange summer things from the piney woods tapped against the screens.

Aunt Dessie said, "Noella's going to be as surprised as I was. I still can't believe I'm riding along beside you, Mary. After seventeen years."

"Is it that long?" my mother said.

Aunt Dessie turned back to me. "And to finally get to see you, pretty thing. The image of your daddy."

"Are you sure this is the road?" my mother said sharply. "We've really got to keep this visit brief."

"Then why don't you stop at that little place up there and let me ask. Some of this backwoods is hazy in my mind."

We stopped. Aunt Dessie unfolded out of the car like a carpenter's ruler, and yanked open the screen door of a little grocery that had been waiting for a customer since the Depression.

I murmured, "Lordy mercy, as they say down here. Are we talking hazy or crazy?"

"That's enough smart lip," my mother warned me. "You be nice to her. She took us in like royalty. She didn't have to."

"If she tells me one more time I look like my daddy—"

"You do."

"I look like me." It mattered that I was my own special leg of the proud unsteady tripod my mother and father and I had always made. "I feel very guess-who's-here-Annabelle."

"Me too, a little. But suddenly I just wanted to see her and your great-aunt Noella again. I've never forgotten how they took me into the family. No questions. No testing. Just welcome." She was silent, remembering. "I guess I needed their blessing, or something. But I can't tell if Dessie knows."

She lifted the hot hair off her coffee-and-cream neck. She had always worn her hair long and straightened, to please my father. Reverse perm after reverse perm. But now the newest inch of it had its own natural crinkle, recording almost to the day, I guess, when they stopped loving each other. Old fears began to press me like fingers finding the deep secret acupressure points of pain. "What do you mean, *if she knows?* What's to know? You're going to patch all this up. Like the other times, and everything's going to be fine again."

She put her hands on the wheel as if she needed to be driving.

"You are," I said.

"Tina, sometimes things—"

"No. You *are.*"

Aunt Dessie came striding out, carrying a piece of paper in one hand and a bright canvas bag in the other.

"Lady in there makes these totes," she announced, handing it to me. "A souvenir."

I took it, surprised. "Thanks," I said, actually smiling in my confusion. Her old eyes studied me so long that I said too loudly, "Hey, I could embroider YUCK! on it and give it to Sharon for a diaper bag."

"Who's Sharon?" Aunt Dessie asked.

My mother started off with a jerk. "A bubble-headed little blonde Tina knows back home."

"Just my best friend," I said.

Aunt Dessie studied the scrap of paper someone had drawn a map on. "Ah," she nodded. "I see."

"Actually," my mother said, her voice accelerating with the car, "she's a strange little person who keeps trying to saddle Tina with all her problems. I hoped this trip would give them a vacation from each other."

Lie, I said to her back. *You'd rather run from that empty-feeling house than face up to your life.*

"She didn't saddle me," I told Aunt Dessie. "Somebody has to look after Sharon, she's so casual, so inconceivably—" I began to giggle crazily and couldn't stop. "I have to remind her what the doctor says to do, or she'll eat like she wants a French-fried baby with diet-cola blood."

"I think we can spare Aunt Dessie the details."

"Hey, all I did was ask if she could stay with us till the

baby comes. And you went off like a ton of dynamite—rip, mangle, roar." My mother's eyes tried to grab mine in the mirror, but I wouldn't look. I wanted to give the details. Hadn't she driven miles out of her way to give her side of things to my father's aunts before he did? Okay, I wanted to tell about my friend who wasn't afraid to gulp down whole chunks of life I hadn't even dared to taste.

She said, "The last thing I need is a tenth-grade dropout with a fatherless child on the way."

"There's always a father," I objected. "She just doesn't want him around." I tried to think what the slang had been in my mother's day. "He's a creep. She doesn't really like him."

"Turn left," Aunt Dessie said. My mother swerved.

"It's the baby that's important," I said. "Sharon's going to have something really truly her very own. She's glad about it."

"My God," my mother said. She bore through a tunnel of pines riddled with sunlight shafts. "But not in my house."

I braced myself carefully. "But she *is* in our house. I gave her the key before we left."

The car lurched to a stop. My mother swung around in her seat. "Tina! You knew perfectly well how I felt about that."

"Where else could she go?"

"Good heavens, she has parents."

"Oh, sure, her mother's in Florida with four stepchildren and her dad got an ultimatum from his girl friend. Who's she supposed to turn to besides us? I'm her friend. I thought you were, too, the way you were always nice to her and laughed when she did weird things—"

Aunt Dessie said firmly, "Left again up there at that tree."

My mother started the car and drove past a field of sunflowers all staring at us with little happy faces. Slowly tears as hard as hailstones filled my throat. "I thought I could depend on you," I said, bumping along like the car.

"To help her. But you slide out of things like a plate of noodles."

Aunt Dessie said, "I gather your daddy's away from home."

"He still travels, you know," my mother answered for me. "In his kind of work he has to, a great deal."

She slowed as the rutted road dipped for a creek. A little boy in overalls stood expectantly beside a mailbox. Suddenly I knew how my father had looked, growing up in those piney woods. Waiting for the mail carrier to come with something wonderful. I snapped my eyes shut to block him off. I didn't want to think about my father. I didn't even know how to think about him anymore. I just wanted everything to stand still, frozen like that little boy, so that nothing would ever have to arrive.

"How long has he been dead?" I heard my mother say. I jerked to attention, but she added, "Noella's husband."

"I guess two years now," Aunt Dessie said. "Bless her heart, it must be hard for her." She turned around in the seat, raising her voice in case I had gone deaf. "Noella's husband was your Granddaddy Mayhew's brother, you see, and I'm from your grandmother's side, so Noella and I aren't anything like blood kin."

My mother said, "Why have you kept up with each other all these years?"

Aunt Dessie craned to read the name of a small wooden church we were passing. "I guess we just feel related." She turned back to me. "Your daddy stayed with me four years, so he could be close to a better school. I loved that boy."

I gazed at the crooked rows of her gray hair, wondering what age she had been when she stared into a mirror at her horse face and rawboned body and knew no man was ever going to love her.

We passed a square unpainted house smothering under a trumpet vine. "Whoa!" Aunt Dessie commanded. "It says Mayhew on the mailbox."

"This is it?" My mother stopped and backed up. At the

side of a barn two pigs lay in a juicy wallow. Some little
granny in clodhopper shoes just had to be around the
corner, stewing the wash in a black pot. "Good heavens,"
she murmured. "I wouldn't live out here all alone for the
world."

"Well, Noella's not alone, you remember. She's still got
Arley with her." Aunt Dessie flipped her stiff old hand at a
hill nearby. "And the old Mayhew cemetery's up there.
There's family around."

We stopped in front of the house. The screen opened
and a little dried-apple woman came to the edge of the
porch. Aunt Dessie unfolded and strode up the steps into
her arms.

"Who do you think I brought to see you, Noella?" she
demanded. "Here's Jimmie's wife. Mary."

Jimmie? I thought. My father could never have been
anyone but James. Cool upwardly mobile James.

"Of course it's Mary," Noella said in a quavery voice as
tender as cake. "You precious thing. I'm so thankful to see
you again." She wound her arms around my mother like
roots.

Aunt Dessie said, "And this is Jimmie's daughter. This is
Tina." Then I was inside that root-hold, as helpless as a
rock being broken by long gentle pressure.

"I would have known you," Noella said. I braced myself.
"You have his face, your daddy's face. I always hoped I'd
get to see you." She looked beyond me at the empty car.

My mother looked, too, as if she had just recalled the
trips we used to take when my father would wake up in
the back seat, yelling, "Hey, we've *arrived*—why didn't
you tell me?" while we laughed. "James would have liked
to come, I'm sure. But he's a busy man these days."

Noella took her arm. "Tell him I miss him."

"Yes," my mother said, glancing sharply at me to make
sure I didn't blurt out, *How can she tell him when he
moved out a month ago?*

We sat in Noella's cramped little living room while she
slushed around in her slippers, bringing us iced tea. She

and Aunt Dessie took big breaths and brought each other up-to-date on who had died since they last visited. They made me nervous, reminding me how life changes and the people we love fall away.

I stared out the window through a bouquet of plastic flowers that was never going to die. All at once I realized that a man's bearded face was staring in at me.

I screamed, giving a start that filled my lap with iced tea.

Noella said calmly, "It's just Arley, precious. He wants to see who you are, but he's shy." The face scowled, punctured by a gaping mouth, and disappeared. She patted my skirt with everyone's pink paper napkins and sent me out into the sun to dry.

Aunt Dessie strolled out behind me. "Who's Arley?" I whispered, afraid I'd see that face again peeking through the beanpoles of the garden.

"Noella's son," Aunt Dessie said.

"But he's middle-aged." It sounded stupid, but I couldn't recall ever seeing a retarded adult. I guess I thought they stayed children.

"Of course he is. We grow, whether we're ready or not. We do the best we can." She picked a skinny red-pepper pod and bit off the end. "Mercy! Jalapeño." She fanned her tongue.

We walked along the garden rows while my skirt dried. Behind a hedge a bear-shaped shadow stayed even with us.

"Your mother seems very sad," Aunt Dessie said.

I shrugged. "Really?" Suddenly it would have been a relief to pour out the whole They've-split-again-and-it's-awful-and-I'm-scared story.

"Trouble at home?"

I kept shrugging. "Not exactly. Well, maybe a little, but they'll work it out. They always do."

"Ah," Aunt Dessie said.

When we went into the kitchen, my mother was setting plates around a table that practically sagged under bowls of macaroni and cheese and sliced tomatoes and fried okra and chowchow and peaches that perfumed the room. All at once I was famished.

Noella piled food on a tray and took it to the door, saying, "Arley wants to eat on the porch. It takes him a little while to get used to new people."

I stuffed myself. Aunt Dessie kept right up with me, begging her gall bladder to forgive and forget. My mother ate in silence, watching the two old faces opposite her like a play.

Noella said, "The last time Dessie came for a visit she brought me the most beautiful crocheted bedspread you ever set eyes on. I'll show it to you. Are you still doing bedspreads?"

"Can't afford the thread anymore," Aunt Dessie said. "Now it's bootees and little sacques and caps. I sell some for baby showers and give the rest away to whoever's expecting."

Noella asked, "What kind of projects keep you busy, Mary?"

My mother opened her mouth and nothing came out. I waited with them, curious. *Tell them your hobby is collecting little keys that lock out the things in your life that scare you. And lock you in.*

A glass shattered out on the porch. We jumped again as something crashed against the wall. A blubbering growl rose and faded as footsteps pounded off the porch and away.

Noella took a broom and went out. We waited. My mother pressed a careful furrow in her food and we all studied it like a divination. She asked, "Who will take care of him when she dies?"

Aunt Dessie nodded, musing. "Yes. When he's alone. She worries terribly about that."

Unexpectedly my mother reached across the table and laid her hand on Aunt Dessie's. Aunt Dessie put her other hand on top of theirs and we all looked at the funny fragile layers of hands until Noella came back with the tray full of spilled food and broken glass.

In the hurting silence I found myself offering to do the dishes while they visited, but Noella shooed us out, saying she could do dishes when she didn't have us. I hung at the kitchen door, feeling somehow drawn to her, as she put up the food. "I'm sorry I screamed," I said. "I didn't know."

"Of course you didn't, sugar." She took a dozen gorgeous peaches off the windowsill and put them in a sack. "When Arley was little and I finally knew he was never going to be right, I screamed too. Screamed and screamed." She put the sack into my hands. "Take these with you. Your mother said you're on your way to see her folks."

I wished she hadn't reminded me. "She never did this before." As if I had taken the bottom piece of fruit out of the pyramid at the market, everything began to tumble. "Left home, I mean. To go talk to her folks about it. Like this time it was—it was—" I felt silly tripping over a simple word like *serious*.

"Bless your heart," Noella said.

When we went into the living room, Aunt Dessie asked us, "We do have time to go up to the cemetery a minute, don't we?"

My mother shook her head. "I'm afraid it's getting—"

"We have time," I said. I offered my arm to Noella and we went out past my mother's surprised face.

She and Aunt Dessie followed us up a shade-spattered road to the top of the hill. Noella opened a gate in a wire fence and let us into the little graveyard filled with dark cedars. "Used to be a church here, at the beginning," she said. I looked around, wondering why I had wanted so suddenly and urgently, back at the house, to stand up there with my kin.

Noella led us through the high weeds to a grave with a neat concrete cover. A jar with the stem of a rose in it stood beside the nameplate. Dried petals lay around it. "Arley comes," Noella said.

Aunt Dessie pulled two weeds and brushed the nameplate with their leafy tops. "He was a good kind man, Noella." They looked down in silence. "You were fortunate."

"Oh, yes," Noella said, and put her thin arm through Aunt Dessie's bony one.

My mother walked slowly away toward a worn stone. Years of wind had scoured off all the inscription except one line. It said, *beloved wife of.*

She began to cry, with the loud surprised sound of an animal in pain.

"Oh, precious," Noella exclaimed. "Are you sick?"

My mother pivoted blindly into Aunt Dessie's arms. A sob broke through her fingers. They both caught her tight, not understanding. But I knew.

Fear froze me. My voice made a long arc. "Nooo—you can fix it, you can work it out, you're adults!"

My mother's head rocked back and forth, her long hair sliding.

"Oh, Mary," Aunt Dessie said. "No hope at all?"

"No hope," my mother sobbed.

"What?" Noella asked. "What?"

"The marriage," Aunt Dessie said. "Over."

I whirled and ran. Before the fact could touch me. Over the humps of graves lost in the weeds. "No!" I insisted, with every gasp of breath.

But I knew the fact was right behind me, riding piggyback the way it always had, and there was no way I could ever run fast enough. My father had escaped. Oh, God, I knew it wasn't his fault that he had to keep growing. Out of the piney woods. Out of a marriage with somebody who was growing at a different speed. But I wished I could have hunted for that little boy he had been once, and coaxed him out, and made friends with him.

The fence loomed up. I grabbed the rusty wire and

hung over it, listening to myself gulping air as though nothing in me had died.

When I lifted my head, a hand was reaching toward me from behind a gravestone. I recoiled into the weeds before I saw that it was holding out a yellow flower.

Arley peeped out. "I'm nice," he whispered. "Don't cry." His soft wet mouth crumpled with anxiety. "I don't scare you." He pushed the flower closer.

I cringed away before I could stop myself. He did scare me. All the things I didn't understand scared me. Losing the people I had belonged to. Letting a special person change my life someday. Or mess it up, the way Sharon had let someone mess up hers. I had collected as many keys as my mother to lock the changes out.

Carefully, Arley sniffed the flower to show me what he wanted me to do. He held it out again, smiling, with pollen on his nose.

"Don't cry," he begged. "I'm nice." He had my father's deep eyes. The family face. Mine.

"I know," I said shakily. I could see he was. A big, bearded man-child distressed to see me sad. "It's not you." A year's collection of tears tried to burst out, sweeping my breath away again. I pointed up the hill. "It's that."

He looked up and nodded solemnly, as if he knew all about divorces, and all about the key I'd given Sharon so she'd hang out at our house like always and teach me to be brave. He smiled as if he could explain why people kept rearranging themselves into families so they could take care of each other.

I looked up the slope. My mother was walking toward me, between Aunt Dessie and Noella. Her face was calm. She held their hands. She would cut her hair, I thought. She would let it go natural.

Slowly I reached out and took Arley's flower.

I wondered if he would nod if I suddenly said that, in spite of everything, I knew I was lucky. Lucky to be able to go on from this, without too much to handle like Sharon, or starting from scratch like my mother.

Noella came to me and held me close in her root arms. She gave me a brisk pat. "I don't have a brain cell working. I forgot to show you Dessie's bedspread."

We went through the gate and down the road again. Behind me, my mother said, "Tina?" I felt the tips of her fingers brush my back. "If you're giving Sharon the diaper bag, maybe I could give her some bootees."

I stumbled around to look at her. My voice wiggled as I said, "Would you? It would mean a lot."

Aunt Dessie smiled. "What color shall they be, for this modern little mother? Purple, with orange ribbons?"

"Just a nice traditional white, I would think," my mother said. "Some things don't change."

OUIDA SEBESTYEN

Ouida Sebestyen's fine writing style and sensitive characters were obvious from her first published novel, *Words by Heart,* which was named one of the year's Ten Best by *Learning* magazine and a Best Book of 1979 by *The New York Times.* The book deals with the hope as well as the agony of being a young black girl in 1910 Texas. *Words by Heart* also received the 1982 American Book Award for best children's fiction in paperback.

The success of that novel came after more than twenty years of writing and not selling dozens of stories, four other novels, and a play. But Sebestyen's success with *Words by Heart* continued with *Far from Home,* the touching story of a thirteen-year-old boy's struggle to care for his great-grandmother after his mother dies. *Far from Home* was named Best Book for Young Adults in 1980 by the American Library Association.

IOU's, Ouida Sebestyen's third novel for young adults, is also about love and caring within a splintered family. In *IOU's,* thirteen-year-old Stowe Garrett and his mother work to make a life together after Stowe's grandfather has disowned them and his father has deserted them.

Like "Welcome," all of Sebestyen's stories end on a warm, upbeat note. Also like "Welcome," much of her writing reflects her own Southern heritage and early life in a small Texas town. Raised in Vernon, Texas, she eventually moved to Boulder, Colorado, where she has raised a teenage son while enjoying plants and animals as well as life in the shadow of the Rocky Mountains.

What would you do if you suspected that one of your teachers was someone only disguised as a teacher? What if you discovered he or she was a psychiatric researcher . . . or a spy . . . or someone from another planet? . . .

FUTURE TENSE

ROBERT LIPSYTE

Gary couldn't wait for tenth grade to start so he could strut his sentences, parade his paragraphs, renew his reputation as the top creative writer in school. At the opening assembly, he felt on edge, psyched, like a boxer before the first-round bell. He leaned forward as Dr. Proctor, the principal, introduced two new staff members. He wasn't particularly interested in the new vice-principal, Ms. Jones; Gary never had discipline problems, he'd never even had to stay after school. But his head cocked alertly as Dr. Proctor introduced the new Honors English teacher, Mr. Smith. Here was the person he'd have to impress.

He studied Mr. Smith. The man was hard to describe. He looked as though he'd been manufactured to fit his name. Average height, brownish hair, pale white skin, medium build. Middle age. He was the sort of person you began to forget the minute you met him. Even his clothes had no particular style. They merely covered his body.

Mr. Smith was . . . just there.

Gary was studying Mr. Smith so intently that he didn't hear Dr. Proctor call him up to the stage to receive an award from last term. Jim Baggs jabbed an elbow into his ribs and said, "Let's get up there, Dude."

Dr. Proctor shook Gary's hand and gave him the

County Medal for Best Composition. While Dr. Proctor was giving Jim Baggs the County Trophy for Best All-Round Athlete, Gary glanced over his shoulder to see if Mr. Smith looked impressed. But he couldn't find the new teacher. Gary wondered if Mr. Smith was so ordinary he was invisible when no one was talking about him.

On the way home, Dani Belzer, the prettiest poet in school, asked Gary, "What did you think of our new Mr. Wordsmith?"

"If he was a color he'd be beige," said Gary. "If he was a taste he'd be water. If he was a sound he'd be a low hum."

"Fancy, empty words," sneered Mike Chung, ace reporter on the school paper. "All you've told me is you've got nothing to tell me."

Dani quickly stepped between them. "What did you think of the first assignment?"

"Describe a Typical Day at School," said Gary, trying unsuccessfully to mimic Mr. Smith's bland voice. "That's about as exciting as tofu."

"A real artist," said Dani, "accepts the commonplace as a challenge."

That night, hunched over his humming electric typewriter, Gary wrote a description of a typical day at school from the viewpoint of a new teacher who was seeing everything for the very first time, who took nothing for granted. He described the shredded edges of the limp flag outside the dented front door, the worn flooring where generations of kids had nervously paced outside the principal's office, the nauseatingly sweet pipe-smoke seeping out of the teachers' lounge.

And then, in the last line, he gave the composition that extra twist, the little kicker on which his reputation rested. He wrote:

The new teacher's beady little eyes missed nothing, for they were the optical recorders of an alien creature

who had come to earth to gather information.

The next morning, when Mr. Smith asked for a volun-
teer to read aloud, Gary was on his feet and moving toward the front of the classroom before Mike Chung got his
hand out of his pocket.

The class loved Gary's composition. They laughed and
stamped their feet. Chung shrugged, which meant he
couldn't think of any criticism, and Dani flashed thumbs
up. Best of all, Jim Baggs shouldered Gary against the
blackboard after class and said, "Awesome tale, Dude."

Gary felt good until he got the composition back. Along
one margin, in a perfect script, Mr. Smith had written:

You can do better.

"How would he know?" Gary complained on the way
home.

"You should be grateful," said Dani. "He's pushing you
to the farthest limits of your talent."

"Which may be nearer than you think," snickered
Mike.

Gary rewrote his composition, expanded it, complicated it, thickened it. Not only was this new teacher an
alien, he was part of an extraterrestrial conspiracy to take
over Earth. Gary's final sentence was:

> Every iota of information, frag-
> ment of fact, morsel of minutiae
> sucked up by those vacuuming eyes was
> beamed directly into a computer cir-
> cling the planet. The data would
> eventually become a program that
> would control the mind of every
> school kid on earth.

Gary showed the new draft to Dani before class. He
stood on tiptoes so he could read over her shoulder. Sometimes he wished she were shorter, but mostly he wished
he were taller.

"What do you think?"

"The assignment was to describe a typical day," said Dani. "This is off the wall."

He snatched the papers back. "Creative writing means creating." He walked away, hurt and angry. He thought: *If she doesn't like my compositions, how can I ever get her to like me?*

That morning, Mike Chung read his own composition aloud to the class. He described a typical day through the eyes of a student in a wheelchair. Everything most students take for granted was an obstacle: the bathroom door too heavy to open, the gym steps too steep to climb, the light switch too high on the wall. The class applauded and Mr. Smith nodded approvingly. Even Gary had to admit it was really good—if you considered plain-fact journalism as creative writing, that is.

Gary's rewrite came back the next day marked:

Improving. Try again.

Saturday he locked himself in his room after breakfast and rewrote the rewrite. He carefully selected his nouns and verbs and adjectives. He polished and arranged them in sentences like a jeweler strings pearls. He felt good as he wrote, as the electric typewriter hummed and buzzed and sometimes coughed. He thought: *Every champion knows that as hard as it is to get to the top, it's even harder to stay up there.*

His mother knocked on his door around noon. When he let her in, she said, "It's a beautiful day."

"Big project," he mumbled. He wanted to avoid a distracting conversation.

She smiled. "If you spend too much time in your room, you'll turn into a mushroom."

He wasn't listening. "Thanks. Anything's okay. Don't forget the mayonnaise."

Gary wrote:

```
The alien's probes trembled as he
read the student's composition.
```

```
Could that skinny, bespectacled
earthling really suspect its extra-
terrestrial identity? Or was his
composition merely the result of a
creative thunderstorm in a brilliant
young mind?
```

Before Gary turned in his composition on Monday morning, he showed it to Mike Chung. He should have known better.

"You're trying too hard," chortled Chung. "Truth is stronger than fiction."

Gary flinched at that. It hurt. It might be true. But he couldn't let his competition know he had scored. "You journalists are stuck in the present and the past," growled Gary. "Imagination prepares us for what's going to happen."

Dani read her composition aloud to the class. It described a typical day from the perspective of a louse choosing a head of hair to nest in. The louse moved from the thicket of a varsity crew-cut to the matted jungle of a sagging perm to a straight, sleek blond cascade.

The class cheered and Mr. Smith smiled. Gary felt a twinge of jealousy. Dani and Mike were coming on. There wasn't room for more than one at the top.

In the hallway, he said to Dani, "And you called my composition off the wall?"

Mike jumped in. "There's a big difference between poetical metaphor and hack science fiction."

Gary felt choked by a lump in his throat. He hurried away.

Mr. Smith handed back Gary's composition the next day marked:

See me after school.

Gary was nervous all day. What was there to talk about? Maybe Mr. Smith hated science fiction. One of those traditional English teachers. Didn't understand that science fiction could be literature. *Maybe I can educate him,* thought Gary.

When Gary arrived at the English office, Mr. Smith seemed nervous too. He kept folding and unfolding Gary's composition. "Where do you get such ideas?" he asked in his monotone voice.

Gary shrugged. "They just come to me."

"Alien teachers. Taking over the minds of schoolchildren." Mr. Smith's empty eyes were blinking. "What made you think of that?"

"I've always had this vivid imagination."

"If you're sure it's just your imagination." Mr. Smith looked relieved. "I guess everything will work out." He handed back Gary's composition. "No more fantasy, Gary. Reality. That's your assignment. Write only about what you know."

Outside school, Gary ran into Jim Baggs, who looked surprised to see him. "Don't tell me you had to stay after, Dude."

"I had to see Mr. Smith about my composition. He didn't like it. Told me to stick to reality."

"Don't listen." Jim Baggs body checked Gary into the schoolyard fence. "Dude, you got to be yourself."

Gary ran all the way home and locked himself into his room. He felt feverish with creativity. Dude, you got to be yourself, Dude. It doesn't matter what your so-called friends say, or your English teacher. You've got to play your own kind of game, write your own kind of stories.

The words flowed out of Gary's mind and through his fingers and out of the machine and onto sheets of paper. He wrote and rewrote until he felt the words were exactly right:

```
With great effort, the alien shut
down the electrical panic impulses
coursing through its system and
turned on Logical Overdrive. There
were two possibilities:
```

1. This high school boy was exactly
what he seemed to be, a brilliant,
imaginative, apprentice best-sell-
ing author and screenwriter, or,

2. He had somehow stumbled onto the
secret plan and he would have to be
either enlisted into the conspiracy
or erased off the face of the planet.

First thing in the morning, Gary turned in his new
rewrite to Mr. Smith. A half hour later, Mr. Smith called
Gary out of Spanish. There was no expression on his regular features. He said, "I'm going to need some help with
you."

Cold sweat covered Gary's body as Mr. Smith grabbed
his arm and led him to the new vice-principal. She read
the composition while they waited. Gary got a good look
at her for the first time. Ms. Jones was . . . just there. She
looked as though she'd been manufactured to fit her
name. Average. Standard. Typical. The cold sweat turned
into goose pimples.

How could he have missed the clues? Smith and Jones
were aliens! He had stumbled on their secret and now
they'd have to deal with him.

He blurted, "Are you going to enlist me or erase me?"

Ms. Jones ignored him. "In my opinion, Mr. Smith, you
are overreacting. This sort of nonsense"—she waved
Gary's composition—"is the typical response of an over-
stimulated adolescent to the mixture of reality and fantasy
in an environment dominated by manipulative music,
television, and films. Nothing for us to worry about."

"If you're sure, Ms. Jones," said Mr. Smith. He didn't
sound sure.

The vice-principal looked at Gary for the first time.
There was no expression in her eyes. Her voice was flat.
"You'd better get off this science fiction kick," she said. "If
you know what's good for you."

"I'll never tell another human being, I swear," he babbled.

"What are you talking about?" asked Ms. Jones.

"Your secret is safe with me," he lied. He thought, *If I can just get away from them. Alert the authorities. Save the planet.*

"You see," said Ms. Jones, "you're writing yourself into a crazed state."

"You're beginning to believe your own fantasies," said Mr. Smith.

"I'm not going to do anything this time," said Ms. Jones, "but you must promise to write only about what you know."

"Or I'll have to fail you," said Mr. Smith.

"For your own good," said Ms. Jones. "Writing can be very dangerous."

"Especially for writers," said Mr. Smith, "who write about things they shouldn't."

"Absolutely," said Gary, "positively, no question about it. Only what I know." He backed out the door, nodding his head, thinking, *Just a few more steps and I'm okay. I hope these aliens can't read minds.*

Jim Baggs was practicing head fakes in the hallway. He slammed Gary into the wall with a hip block. "How's it going, Dude?" he asked, helping Gary up.

"Aliens," gasped Gary. "Told me no more science fiction."

"They can't treat a star writer like that," said Jim. "See what the head honcho's got to say." He grabbed Gary's wrist and dragged him to the principal's office.

"What can I do for you, boys?" boomed Dr. Proctor.

"They're messing with his moves, Doc," said Jim Baggs. "You got to let the aces run their races."

"Thank you, James." Dr. Proctor popped his forefinger at the door. "I'll handle this."

"You're home free, Dude," said Jim, whacking Gary across the shoulder blades as he left.

"From the beginning," ordered Dr. Proctor. He nodded sympathetically as Gary told the entire story, from the opening assembly to the meeting with Mr. Smith and Ms. Jones. When Gary was finished, Dr. Proctor took the papers from Gary's hand. He shook his head as he read Gary's latest rewrite.

"You really have a way with words, Gary. I should have sensed you were on to something."

Gary's stomach flipped. "You really think there could be aliens trying to take over Earth?"

"Certainly," said Dr. Proctor, matter-of-factly. "Earth is the ripest plum in the universe."

Gary wasn't sure if he should feel relieved that he wasn't crazy or be scared out of his mind. He took a deep breath to control the quaver in his voice, and said: "I spotted Smith and Jones right away. They look like they were manufactured to fit their names. Obviously humanoids. Panicked as soon as they knew I was on to them."

Dr. Proctor chuckled and shook his head. "No self-respecting civilization would send those two stiffs to Earth."

"They're not aliens?" He felt relieved and disappointed at the same time.

"I checked them out myself," said Dr. Proctor. "Just two average, standard, typical human beings, with no imagination, no creativity."

"So why'd you hire them?"

Dr. Proctor laughed. "Because they'd never spot an alien. No creative imagination. That's why I got rid of the last vice-principal and the last Honors English teacher. They were giving me odd little glances when they thought I wasn't looking. After ten years on your planet, I've learned to smell trouble."

Gary's spine turned to ice and dripped down the backs of his legs. "You're an alien!"

"Great composition," said Dr. Proctor, waving Gary's papers. "Grammatical, vividly written, and totally accurate."

"It's just a composition," babbled Gary, "made the whole thing up, imagination, you know."

Dr. Proctor removed the face of his wristwatch and began tapping tiny buttons. "Always liked writers. I majored in your planet's literature. Writers are the keepers of the past and the hope of the future. Too bad they cause so much trouble in the present."

"I won't tell anyone," cried Gary. "Your secret's safe with me." He began to back slowly toward the door.

Dr. Proctor shook his head. "How can writers keep secrets, Gary? It's their natures to share their creations with the world." He tapped three times and froze Gary in place, one foot raised to step out the door.

"But it was only a composition," screamed Gary as his body disappeared before his eyes.

"And I can't wait to hear what the folks back home say when you read it to them," said Dr. Proctor.

"I made it all up." Gary had the sensation of rocketing upward. "I made up the whole . . ."

ROBERT LIPSYTE

A former prizewinning sportswriter for *The New York Times,* Robert Lipsyte attracted teen-age readers with his first novel, *The Contender,* a story about a young black boxer trying to find his place in the world. *The Contender* was named a Notable Book for Children by the American Library Association and won the 1967 Children's Book Award from the Child Study Association of America. In addition to writing novels, screenplays, and television scripts, Mr. Lipsyte has published two works of nonfiction: *Assignment: Sports* and *Free to Be Muhammad Ali.* Sports, again, is the central focus of *Jock and Jill,* a young adult novel that deals also with issues of poverty, romance, and personal integrity.

Lipsyte's most familiar character is Bobby Marks, the overweight hero of *One Fat Summer,* a book that was chosen as a Best Book for Young Adults in 1977 and a Best of the Best—1970–1982 by the Young Adult Services Division of the ALA. A trimmer, more self-assured Bobby appears again as a camp counselor in *Summer Rules.* Lipsyte's most recent novel, *Summerboy,* completes the trilogy.

A New Yorker by birth, Mr. Lipsyte now lives in New Jersey with two children and his wife, Marjorie, who is also a writer. Most recently Bob Lipsyte has appeared regularly on network television's CBS News Sunday Morning program as a guest columnist.

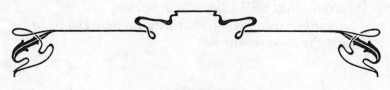

LOVES

Will he call? When will he call? Will that phone ever ring?

And what will I say when he does call?

Being a teen-age girl waiting to be asked out to a party is sooooo painful. . . .

TURMOIL
IN A BLUE AND BEIGE BEDROOM

JUDIE ANGELL

Please let John call.

Please let John call before two o'clock.

If John calls before two o'clock I promise I'll baby-sit Stewie for three Friday nights in a row without arguing.

Now, what will I wear?

I haven't worn my powder blue sweater with the fluffy collar to school yet . . . I could wear that with my tan slacks. Or my black slacks. Or my white wool ones? Maybe I'll wear a dress. . . .

If Claudia goes with Tim, maybe we could double, since Tim drives. . . . Yes! That's a great idea, I'll call Claudia. No, I'll wait until I hear from John.

Please let John call soon! If he calls soon I'll try not to argue about *anything* for two whole weeks. Unless they tell me I have to be home by eleven or something. . . . But I promise, that would be the only argument.

Can I wear my hair a new way? How can I wear my hair a new way when it's so *short!* Maybe I could stick combs in the sides or something, and pull it up over my ears like this. . . . Yuck, too many pictures stuck in the frame of my mirror, I can't even see myself in it anymore. . . .

Mmmm, I should get rid of *this* picture, anyway. Billy and me. Billy's such a creep, how could I ever have liked him? Look at that, he's wearing Bermuda *shorts,* for Lord's sake, what a stupid picture. And there's stupid Kenny Rappoport in the background, holding up two fingers over Billy's head. Why did I even bother to keep such a stupid picture? And look at *me,* with two dumb ponytails sticking out of the sides of my head . . . I look like a cocker spaniel, for Lord's sake! This picture goes *out,* that's it!

Billy. I bet he wasn't even invited to Nancy's party. And if he was invited I bet he goes with *Marcia!* They really deserve each other.

Oh! The phone! It's ringing, it's ring-ing! I'll let it ring again. Four times, so I won't look anxious. Three . . . four . . .

Hel-low?

Oh. Hi, Mom. What do you mean you're surprised you got through? I've hardly been on the phone at *all* today! Are you calling from the dentist's? Did Stewie have any cavities? Well, good. Listen, Mom, I'm kind of waiting for a call, so—What? Did I do the dishes? Well, not yet, but— The what? The kitty litter? I *will,* Mom, but I haven't had a minute—My *bedroom?* It looks *fine,* it doesn't need any cleaning. It does not, Mom! Okay, okay, I will. I *will.* I said I *would,* Mom—*Please* stop saying "all you teen-agers." We are *not* all alike, Mom, in spite of what you parents think! I am not sighing heavily, Mom, and I'll do the stuff, okay? Okay. Bye.

Par-ents!

Now. Where was I?

The party. Clothes.

Maybe I shouldn't wear the powder blue. Practically everything I own is powder blue. I'm almost totally *associated* with powder blue, like a trademark or something. Who needs *that!*

Maybe green. No, green makes my skin look yellow. Maybe *yellow!*

Oooooh, there's the phone again. Two . . . threee . . .

Hel-low?

Oh, it's you, Susan.

No, I'm not disappointed, I thought you were somebody else, that's all. Never *mind* who else. *No*body else, I just didn't expect *you*. No, not Roger. No, not Peter, either. *Nobody*, Susan!

Of *course* not *Allen*, Susan, why would you ever think of Allen? Like gross, Susan! Did anyone say anything to you about me and Allen? Did they? You *swear?*

I am *not* overreacting, I just don't know why you would even imagine I might be expecting a call from Allen, he's so wimpy! And he has that awful growth on his cheek. Well, you can call it a beauty mark, I call it a growth!

Listen, I really can't stand Allen Mitchell and let's change the—John? John Carraro? I am not blushing, Susan, how can you tell, anyway, over the phone?

Okay. Maybe John, but just maybe *maybe*, not really *really.*

Stop laughing, Susan, I just thought that *maybe* if John asked me I might go with him, *maybe.* But I don't know and I'm not counting on it. Who are you going with? You're going *stag?* You're kidding! You *are?* But Nancy said *couples!* She did, I swear, I was standing right there when she invited both of us!

She did say couples, Susan. How could you show up there all by yourself when everyone else will be paired off? Susan, I *heard* her say couples.

Well, I think that's pretty gutsy of you, I really do.

The geometry? No, I haven't looked at it yet, why? Trapezoids? What's a trapezoid, I thought that was an order of monks. No, I must have been absent for that. You will? Oh, Susan, you're a doll, you'll really help me? Thanks, you're the best friend I ever had. Phyllis? She is not my best friend. Well, maybe I did, but not anymore. She told Mary Ann I was a snob, do you believe that? Me, a snob! She's the one who's a snob. Just because she had two dates with a boy from Princeton she wouldn't speak to any high school boy for weeks, practically.

Listen, Susan, Phyllis is the type who doesn't even know the meaning of the word *friendship*. She'll just turn on you for no reason and start saying things behind your back.

Oh, boy, what time is it? It is? Say, I'd better hang up. Stop giggling, Susan, it is not because I'm expecting a call from John. I promised my mother I'd help her. Never mind with *what*, Susan, I have to hang up.

Okay, bye.

I cannot believe Susan would show up at Nancy's party alone! I bet she has a date, she's just not telling me who yet, that's all. Some best friend *she* is. . . .

I am absolutely getting claustrophobic in this room.

I wonder what the other kids are doing?

Are they staying home on a perfectly gorgeous Saturday afternoon waiting for a date for Nancy's party or are they going out?

What I'd really like to do is call Liz or Mary Ann or somebody but I just can't tie up the phone anymore. . . .

If John would just call *now*, then I could get out of this room and get on with my *life!* I am just stagnating and withering away in this *room!*

Call, John, call. Call, John, call. One, two, three, ring!

If John calls now I'll know I was right all along. I am special. I am different. I am leading a charmed life. I will get everything I desperately want because I was born under a lucky star and everything will be perfect and beautiful forever.

Oh, I know *some* bad things will happen, but not really tragic and I will rise above them and be a better person afterward. And the things I really want, the really important things in life, will all be there like a dream come true because I am magic. If I close my eyes and will it strongly enough—

I'll lie flat on my back and close my eyes. Not too tightly. I'll take a deep breath. . . .

Maybe I will actually have an out-of-body experience. Wouldn't that be terrific? You leave your body and soar above it . . . but you're still attached to it by a beautiful silver cord. . . .

Deep breath, dee—eep breath.

Ouch, what's that?

Oh, my nightgown is caught under me. I should have made my bed, it's so uncomfortable on your back when stuff is wrinkled up underneath you. . . .

There. That's better.

Breathe deeply, deeply.

I am living a charmed life. Everything is perfect. John will call and I will go with him to Nancy's party and I will wear powder blue and everything will be perfect. . . .

Inhale, exhale.

Inhale, exhale.

Mmmm. . . .

Thephoneisringing. . . . The *phone?*

Hello?

Oh. Hi, Mary Ann.

My voice sounds as if what? Oh. Well . . . maybe I did doze off for a minute, I've been *so* exhausted lately. You too? I know, isn't it awful?

Nancy's party? I guess so, but I'm not sure. Are you? You are? Who with? By *yourself?* But you're supposed to go with a date. Nancy said so! *She's* going with Bob Reifschneider.

Well, Susan said she's going stag, too, maybe she could be your date.

Oh, I don't know. I'd really feel funny walking in there without a date. Are you really going alone? No, nothing's *wrong* with it. I'd just feel funny, that's all. I mean, I *heard* Nancy say *couples.*

Mary Ann, remember those dumb parties back in junior high where we all went by ourselves and the girls were always on one side of the room and the boys were on the other and how gross and immature it all was?

Yes, I know we're all older now, but still, it would probably end up the same way, don't you think so? That's why

Nancy said "couples" to show we've gotten past those kid games and things.

You really think it would be different now? Oh, I don't know. . . .

Go where? Down to the arcade? Oh . . . gee, I'd really like to . . . but I got behind on my geometry and I have to spend the afternoon grinding away on that. You know, trapezoids and stuff . . .

Okay, thanks anyway. Have a good time. . . . Bye.

Oh, Mary Ann? Call me when you get back and tell me who you saw there, okay? Good. Bye.

Oooooh, that makes me so mad! I *want* to go to the arcade with Mary Ann, I *want* to!

John Carraro, you are ruining my whole afternoon! Will you please just call me so I can unchain myself from this room before my entire life passes by and my hair turns white and falls out?

If Mary Ann is going to the arcade she'll probably see Claudia and maybe Susan and probably Liz and . . . And everyone will be having a perfectly terrific afternoon while I sit here waiting for my date to call!

Of course, it would be okay if he called and I wasn't here and then he'd wonder where I was and all that. . . . Except there isn't a soul in this entire house right now and so I wouldn't get the message. And who knows when and *if* he'd ever call back. Maybe he'd even try someone *else* if he couldn't get me, so no.

No arcade. No terrific afternoon.

Just me and my room.

Wonderful.

Please let John call. Now.

I'm probably going to flunk geometry. Not flunk . . . maybe a D. Mom will die if I get a D. She'll just die. I can't get a D, I just can't. I won't. Susan will help me and I'll get a C. A C isn't so bad. And maybe if I will it strongly enough I'll get a B, especially if I really am living a charmed life.

Maybe I'll put on some records. Good idea! Records will take my mind off everything!

Let's see . . . oh, I'm tired of this one.

This one is boring.

I'm not in the mood for this one. . . .

This one is scratched. I'll *kill* Stewie for coming into this room without permission and touching my things! I'll just kill him! Little brat . . .

This one I always hated. . . .

There's nothing here! This whole record collection is worth squat!

I'd better lie down and close my eyes again and take deep breaths.

I really hate myself when I get like this.

If John would just call I could finally relax.

I mustn't go to sleep, I mustn't go to sleep. I sounded all muzzy before when Mary Ann called and I can't sound like I've been sleeping on a perfectly gorgeous Saturday afternoon. I mean, what would he think, that I had nothing to do on a perfectly gorgeous Saturday afternoon except sleep?

I will not sleep. I'll just concentrate on relaxing.

Call, John, hurry up.

Breathe in, breathe out.

I can't relax, I can't.

I think I'll call Phyllis.

Just for a minute. Just to see what's happening.

Five-five-five, nine-one-eight . . . three. There.

Hello, Mrs. Atwater? Is Phyllis there? This is June. She went to the arcade? Oh. Well, thanks. Uh, no, no message. Bye.

Phyllis is at the arcade, too! Rats! The whole world is down there having the time of their happy little lives and here I sit in this ROOM!

Maybe even *John* is at the arcade!

No, he never goes there. He's so sweet, he always helps out his father on weekends.

Maybe he's too busy with his father to call.

No, if he's home helping his father, he'll call when he

takes his break. I know he will, it will be a perfect time to call.

He's so cute.

He has a beauty mark, too, but it's a nice one. . . .

Aha! The phone! This time I'll give it two rings. Okay. Hel-low?

Oh, hi, Liz.

No, just geometry, what about you?

Mmmm, Mary Ann called me too, but I told her I was going to hang around here. Thanks, anyway.

Nancy's party? Gee, I've hardly even thought about it, why?

Uh. Well, I thought slacks. I mean, it's not formal or anything.

Do I have a date? Well, I don't want to say yet. No, I'm not keeping secrets, honest. I'm just . . . not sure yet. How about you?

Stag? Really, Liz?

Why do you think couples are a dumb idea?

Well, no, I don't think being paired off "inhibits" any-body, I thought it sounded more mature to go with dates for a change. I mean, we've all been in "groups" since first grade, for Lord's sake.

Oh, well, if you think most kids feel more comfortable going stag, then go stag, I mean—you have to feel com-fortable.

Okay, have fun. Bye.

Well.

Nancy will certainly be surprised. I mean, it's *her* party and she should have the right to say how people go to it, after all!

Gosh, why does everything have to get so *complicated?* I mean, I really can't stand it!

Susan is going stag. *Liz* is going stag. Mary *Ann* is going stag. They're going to start an epidemic! I bet now *every-one* will go stag!

Oh, barf *city!* If everyone goes stag, *I'm* sure not going to be the only one with a date, not *me!*

Oh, can you just see how *that* would come off? Everyone laughing and carrying on in cute little groups and I walk in with a date?

Ohhh, no!

Ohmygosh, but what if *John* calls?

What—if—John Carraro calls and asks me to this party that the whole entire *world* is going to *stag!*

I absolutely can't talk to him, I'll have to avoid him!

The first thing to do is get out of this room right now! Where's my comb?

Here I've been sitting around this positively claustrophobic room all afternoon like the biggest fool who ever grew ears while the entire world is downtown at the arcade—

Where *is* my comb?

Oh, no! The phone.

I won't answer it.

I won't.

But what if it's an emergency or something?

Okay, I'll answer it.

H'lo?

Who?

Ohhh!

Hi, John . . .

Me? Well, I just finished *tons* of geometry and I thought I'd treat myself to a trip downtown, you just caught me. . . . I'm on my way out the door. Right now.

No, you're not keeping me, but what? Just one question? Oh, okay . . .

Oh, wow, Nancy's party? Oh, wow, this is really a surprise. . . . Hmmm . . . Wow . . . Well, gee, John, it's awfully nice of you to ask me, I mean, I'm really flattered. . . . But the thing is . . . Well, I was thinking that it could be so much more fun if we all went in a big group, you know, and so no one would feel, you know, inhibited or anything if they didn't have a date, know what I mean? I really do think big groups are so much more congenial, don't you? But, really, John, thanks a lot for asking me, I honestly think it was so nice. Bye, John.

Oh, boy!

Boy!

Now where's that comb?

What—is—*that?* Is that the beginning of a *zit?*

Oh, *please,* don't let me be starting a zit! Please, please, just let my face stay clear and I *promise* I'll catch up on geometry!

JUDIE ANGELL

Judie Angell, a former elementary school teacher, editor for *TV Guide,* and continuity writer for Channel 13, New York City's educational television station, is well-known for her novels for young people. She is the author of *In Summertime It's Tuffy, Tina Gogo, Ronnie and Rosey, A Word from Our Sponsor or My Friend Alfred, Secret Selves, Dear Lola or How to Build Your Own Family, What's Best for You, The Buffalo Nickel Blues Band,* and *Suds.* Her most recent novel, *First the Good News,* deals with the wacky adventures of five high school girls trying to track down a television star to interview him for a school newspaper contest.

Under the name Fran Arrick she has also published several highly praised novels that deal with the harsher aspects of the lives of some teen-agers. Arrick's first novel, *Steffie Can't Come Out to Play,* was named an Outstanding Book for Young Adults by the American Library Association in 1978. That story of a runaway teen-ager who is led into prostitution in New York City was followed by *Tunnel Vision,* one of the ALA's Fifty Best Books, in which several characters—teen-agers as well as adults—examine their past relationship with Anthony, a bright and well-liked fifteen-year-old who has committed suicide. In *Chernowitz!* a teen-ager in a small community has to confront anti-Semitism spread by a vicious bully in his school. Fran Arrick's most recent novel deals with religious extremism and is called *God's Radar.*

The author lives with her musician husband and two sons in South Salem, New York.

In wartime, every young soldier about to be shipped overseas worries about his uncertain future. What will the war be like? Will he come back alive? Will his girl friend wait for him? Jack Raab isn't even certain he has a girl friend. He had met Dottie only briefly during basic training. He's never even kissed her. And now it's his last day at home. . . .

FURLOUGH—1944

HARRY MAZER

It was during the Second World War, on a Saturday of a bright October morning in 1944, when Jack Raab, flushed and out of breath, met Dottie Landon on the corner of Neptune and Coney Island Avenue. Jack was in his dark winter uniform with the newly-sewn-on corporal's stripes and the silver gunner's wings pinned over his left breast pocket.

Dottie wore a navy pea jacket, a pleated skirt, white ankle socks, and saddle shoes. "I had a big fight with my mother," she said, glancing at Jack then back at the curly-haired boy with her. She seemed ill at ease. "She doesn't like me going out with soldiers."

"She doesn't?" Jack blushed. Had Dottie met him just to tell him she couldn't stay out with him? The pea jacket disturbed him. Maybe she liked sailors more. He hardly knew Dottie. They'd met only once, ten months ago in Miami.

Jack had been in basic training in Florida and Dottie was there on vacation with her parents. They'd met on the beach and struck up a conversation. That is, Dottie had struck up a conversation. She was the talker, the outgoing one—the extrovert. Jack was too shy around girls to say much at all. They were both from New York City, which gave them something in common. They spent the day together, walking up and down the beach.

"We'll meet again," Jack said when they parted. It was his best moment, like Humphrey Bogart in *Casablanca*, but not as sarcastic. Dottie gave him her address and they promised to write.

In the weeks that followed, Jack thought about Dottie all the time, but for a long time he didn't write because the letters he began seemed so babyish. His penmanship only made it worse. He finally printed a stiff little note with little more in it than his new address. He was in Aerial Gunnery School in Nevada and he was thinking about her a lot.

Dottie's first letter was five pages long! He kept it and all the others she wrote him in a White Owl cigar box. Her snapshots he taped under the lid. Dottie wrote that she kept his picture safe under the glass on her dresser. "I can't wait till your furlough," she wrote.

So why hadn't he gone to see her the minute he got into the city? He had been back a week, more than a week in fact, but hadn't gotten up the nerve to call Dottie till this morning. Today was it, the last day of his last furlough before going overseas. "Make hay while the sun shines," his buddy Chuckie had said before they parted. "Once we get over there . . ."

Over there was overseas. That's where the war was. *You might never come back.* The thought was always there in Jack's mind.

He recognized Dottie more from the pictures they'd exchanged than from seeing her. It was her, but she seemed older. It made him even shyer.

"Jack, this is my cousin Greenie," Dottie was saying. "The only good thing about him is he's got a car."

"Is it really yours?" Jack said, and then was sorry. It was such a kid thing to say.

"Everybody thinks they can ride in it anytime they want to," Greenie said. "I used up all my ration stamps this month. Now I'm using kerosene in the motor. It makes the car kick and sputter. And the back tires are extremely bald. I don't dare go over twenty miles an hour."

"My cousin's a worrier. Admit it, Greenie." Dottie pushed her cousin. "Tell him not to worry so much, Jack. He's only sixteen. We're hoping he'll grow out of it."

Jack couldn't think of anything to say. When Dottie laughed, he laughed too, then stuck a cigarette in the corner of his mouth.

Greenie's nose twitched, which made him look a little like a rabbit, a llama, really, with a long, worried, friendly face.

Dottie ruffled Greenie's hair. "He doesn't smoke, Jack. My cousin worries about his health too much. He wants to live forever."

Jack felt a twinge of jealousy. All the time Dottie was talking to him she was pushing and pulling her cousin.

Another girl joined them. "This is Selma." She wore a navy pea jacket identical to Dottie's.

"A corporal!" Selma said, opening her arms wide. "You're always so *lucky,* Dottie. Where'd you find a beauty-full soldier like this?" Selma said everything in such an enthusiastic way that Jack liked her immediately.

"Hey, Jerry! Lil! Meyer!" Selma hollered to some kids on the street. "Come on over and meet a soldier. We'll all go for a ride."

Greenie nearly choked. "My tires can't take all that load. You know how hard it is to get a tire?"

"You and your tires." Selma winked at Jack. "We'll ride on the rims if we have to."

Jack fell silent when the others appeared. Dottie kept glancing at him. He furrowed his brow and tried to look calm and dependable like Gary Cooper.

They all piled into the car. "Seven's too much," Greenie said.

"Three in front, the rest in back," Selma said briskly. "Double up in back. Nobody gets left out. You, Dottie, sit on Corporal Jack's lap. You lucky thing." She climbed in next to Greenie. "Okay now, Greenman, honey, drive."

"Drive where? I don't want to drive anywhere."

"Just drive," Selma said. "I'll think of something."

Dottie sat gingerly on Jack's lap. "I'm too heavy for you."

"No, you're not." He pulled her back. He didn't know where he got the nerve.

"You're crushing me."

"Sorry." He straightened up, feeling both excited and alarmed. He had never had a real date in his life.

Selma turned around to smile at Jack in back. "Cozy? Who's got a ciggy?"

Jack slid around to get his pack and offered cigarettes all around. Jerry and Meyer lit up. Lil and Dottie didn't smoke.

They rode through the park, screaming as the car went around curves. "I'm hungry," Lil said. She took out her lipstick and reddened her mouth.

"We'll go to White Castle," Selma said.

Dottie leaned close to Jack. "Do you want to?"

"Sure he wants to," Selma said. "Soldiers are always hungry."

"I wish I was in service," Dottie said softly just for Jack.

"You couldn't stand being in a uniform," Selma said. She heard everything. "You like clothes too much."

"My sister is in the WACs," Lil said. "She likes her uniform."

"That's right," Dottie said. "What do clothes have to do with the real person?"

"Not much," Jack said, "unless you're an officer. I see those bars, I see that silver leaf, I see that star—I salute. If they put a star on a jeep, I salute the jeep. If they put it on a tree, I salute the tree."

Dottie laughed. He'd made her laugh! *I made a girl laugh!* Her teeth on the bottom were crooked and crowded together. Beautiful crooked teeth. Beautiful crooked smile. Beautiful laugh.

Greenie got lost and couldn't find the way out of the park. They drove by the museum three times. Everyone yelled insults at Greenie. "Wrong-way Corrigan . . . Where'd you get your license? . . . Monkey-Wards?" Finally they blundered out of the park onto a street lined with apartment houses and stores.

"Stop on the corner," Meyer ordered. "Forget the hamburgers. Just let me out of this rattletrap. I've got to go home."

"Us, too." Jerry and Lil jumped out.

"You can stay, can't you?" Jack said anxiously to Dottie.

"I can call my mother later."

They all got out of the car now, Selma and Greenie, and Dottie and Jack. "Let's go to the beach and have a picnic," Dottie said. "We'll make a fire and roast hot dogs."

"We'll need mustard, paper plates, Cokes, marshmallows, and beer for Jack." Selma put a hand out for money and Jack gave her a five-dollar bill. "Sport," Selma said, and she and Greenie went to do the shopping.

Dottie leaned against the fender, hands in her pea jacket pockets. Jack leaned on the car next to her. It was the first time they had been alone together. She wasn't talking. He wasn't talking. Somebody had to say something.

"You having a good time? I'm having a swell time." She held out her hand and he caught it and pulled her around. The movement, swinging her around was almost like Fred Astaire and Ginger Rogers, the two of them dancing, he in his top hat and she in a swirly white gown.

In the car again, they all squeezed into the front seat together. "Cozy," Selma said. Her legs were pressed against Jack's. He couldn't help looking and then he felt like a pervert because Dottie was his girl.

At Coney Island they parked under the boardwalk and carried everything across the sand toward the ocean. Selma's shoes kept filling up with sand. Every few steps she leaned on Jack to empty them. Greenie and Dottie went ahead with the supplies.

When they got to the water, Greenie was gathering driftwood for the fire. Dottie was way out on the stone breakwater. Jack climbed out to join her. Dottie was picking up worn bits of pebbles and glass.

"I like weathered things, don't you?" she said.

"Weathered things are great," Jack said, relieved that she wasn't mad at him for staying back with Selma. The ocean rose and fell around them. Seaweed and shells stirred in the sand. Jack wedged a piece of driftwood between the rocks and made a place where they could sit out of the wind. Out here on the rocks it was like being in the middle of the ocean cut off from everyone.

Dottie remembered the day they'd spent on the beach in Miami. "Water is destined to play a part in our lives," she said, linking them so simply, so perfectly.

He could never put what he was feeling into words that well. He wanted to kiss her, but he didn't know how she'd take it. He pressed her hand fervently.

The wind was so strong they had to lean their heads together to talk. "It's amazing how we like the same things," she said. "The ocean and the outdoors—We're so much alike. You're quiet around people. I am too. When I talk a lot it's only because I'm nervous."

When they joined Selma and Greenie, the hot dogs were roasting on the fire. Selma handed Jack an open bottle of beer. "Deluxe service."

Dottie sipped Jack's beer. "I like it, I guess."

"You have to develop a taste for it," Jack said knowingly. He'd only recently developed a taste for beer himself.

When the sun went down, they carried everything back to the car. Jack didn't want the day to end. Tomorrow he'd be on the train on his way back to camp. "Should we stay?" He pulled Dottie aside. "Can you?" They exchanged a look. Selma and Greenie were in the car already. "It's my last day."

"Your last day! I thought your furlough just started."

"No, I—" He shook his head. "I should have called—"

"Your last day!"

"I was afraid you wouldn't want to see me that much."

"How could you think that? Oh, Jack, only one day. Are you really going tomorrow?" She pushed his shoulder. "I could kill you, Jack."

Jack smiled sheepishly. He was dismayed and happy both. One day, a week, that was the way the war was. There was no time, never enough time. *Make hay while the sun shines.* "A lot can happen in one day," he said and let his eyelids fall like Charles Boyer.

Dottie walked back to the car. "We're going to stay for a while," she said to her cousin.

"How are you going to get back?"

"Bus, dumbo. Tell my mother I'll be home later."

Selma stuck her head out the car window and rolled her eyes. "Safe with the U.S. Army. Don't do anything I wouldn't do."

Alone, they took off their shoes and socks. Jack rolled up his pants and tied their shoes together over his shoulder. The air was cool, but the sand was still warm. They walked along the polished shore, throwing their heads back to look up at the sky.

Partway down the beach they found a lifeguard platform on its side. Together, they righted it and climbed up to the seat. It was cooler now. Jack put his arm around Dottie. She leaned against his shoulder. The wind had died down and the waves broke regularly along the shore.

Out there, beyond the horizon, on the other side of the water, was the war. The long breakers crashed on the shore like guns. In a few days he'd be in England. It didn't seem so far away anymore.

"The ocean keeps coming and coming," he said. "It never ends, does it? It makes you think about your own life—and the end of things."

"Promise me you'll be careful," she said.

He should kiss her now. Tomorrow was too late. He bent toward her and kissed her full on the mouth. At the last moment he was filled with doubt. Were his lips greasy? Did his breath smell of cigarettes and beer? He should have chewed some Wrigley's gum.

"Oh, Jack, I don't want you to go!" She kissed him passionately.

He pressed hard against her. "Let's stay up all night."

"My mother—no, I couldn't, but I don't have to go home for a while yet."

They kissed for a long time. Jack's lips were hot and swollen. His hands slipped under her jacket. Dottie held his hands. "We should be going," she said.

A shiver shook Jack. Going meant good-bye. He didn't know when he'd come back. If he'd come back. It made him angry, and he dared to move his hand over her shoulders and down the front of her blouse. She pushed his hand away.

He wanted more, kisses and more than kisses. How? Where? He didn't know anything, but he should try. *If at first you don't succeed, try and try again.* Chuckie would.

"Stop. I mean it, Jack."

He looked out over the water. Did she know what was over there? Everything was so peaceful here. Did she think this was the whole world? Planes were being shot down over there. Soldiers were dying. He and Chuckie had talked about it a lot. If it was your time, that was it. There was no use thinking about it, but he did, all the time. What if this was his last chance? What if he died and never had another chance? Died a virgin. He kissed Dottie hard on the mouth. "My last night," he said.

Slowly he opened his hands then closed them. "How would it be—" He cleared his throat. "What I mean is, would you—do you know what I'm saying? You and me— Do you—?"

What a mess he made of everything. Chuckie wouldn't talk so much. Didn't she know what he meant! "What would you think if I—I—If we—if you and me—if we went someplace . . ."

"What?"

Why was she so thick? What was he supposed to do, tell

her everything? "Tomorrow, I'll be gone," he said. "I could be killed. I probably will be."

She drew in her lower lip. In the dark her face shone, pale somehow, mysterious and tender. He saw that she understood. They climbed down from the platform. "Where?" she said.

"Here?" he said.

"Okay."

They knelt in the damp sand. She removed her pea jacket and spread it on the ground then sat there, shivering. He put his jacket over her shoulders. "Do you want to? Do you really?"

She threw her arms around him. "Yes, for you—" She made a sound against his neck. "Just for you. I never have."

"Just for me?"

"Yes."

His face swelled with emotion. He thought he might cry. "You don't really want to—? Then we won't," he said and felt like Clark Gable masterfully reassuring the trembling young girl.

They took the bus to Dottie's street. Jack laughed a lot and talked about the future. "Will you write to me overseas?"

"Every day," she promised.

He gave her a miniature pair of gunner's wings. She said she'd wear them everywhere. She was his girl. They were in love again when they parted.

HARRY MAZER

Harry Mazer has worked as a longshoreman, a bus driver, a gandy dancer, and a high school teacher, with degrees from Union College and Syracuse University. He is the author of *Guy Lenny*, a tender story about a sensitive boy living with his divorced father; *The War on Villa Street*, about a young man who loves to run but seems to be running away from his problems at home, especially from his alcoholic father; and *The Dollar Man*, about an overweight teen-ager who tries to establish contact with the father who left home years earlier.

Action plays a large part in three of Mazer's novels. In *Snow Bound*—the film of which has appeared on NBC-TV —a teen-age boy and girl are trapped in a car on a wilderness road by a blizzard. *The Solid Gold Kid*, which he wrote with his wife, Norma Fox Mazer, follows the painful adventures of several teen-agers who are held captive by ruthless kidnappers. In *The Island Keeper*, an overprotected teen-age girl runs away to a small island in a large Canadian lake where she learns to survive on her own.

Mr. Mazer says that his teen-age experiences with girls— or rather lack of them—provided the background feelings that went into writing *I Love You, Stupid!* It's a very funny story about a seventeen-year-old boy with only one thought on his mind, trying desperately to understand the difference between sex, love, and friendship. Mazer's youthful experiences in World War II are reflected in his autobiographical novel, *The Last Mission*. Jack Raab, the main character in "Furlough—1944," is the same individual whose plane is shot down over Czechoslovakia in *The Last Mission*.

Harry Mazer grew up in New York City and now lives with his wife, Norma, in Jamestown, New York.

John isn't sure how to relate to girls. What's worse, he has thoughts he knows he shouldn't have. Being a teen-ager in his kind of society is becoming increasingly difficult. He may even be on the brink of losing control. . . .

DO YOU WANT MY OPINION?

M. E. KERR

The night before last I dreamed that Cynthia Slater asked my opinion of *The Catcher in the Rye*.

Last night I dreamed I told Lauren Lake what I thought about John Lennon's music, Picasso's art, and Soviet-American relations.

It's getting worse.

I'm tired of putting my head under the cold-water faucet.

Early this morning my father came into my room and said, "John, are you getting serious with Eleanor Rossi?"

"Just because I took her out three times?"

"Just because you sit up until all hours of the night talking with her!" he said. "We know all about it, John. Her mother called your mother."

I didn't say anything. I finished getting on my socks and shoes.

He was standing over me, ready to deliver the lecture.

It always started the same way.

"You're going to get in trouble if you're intimate, John. You're too young to let a girl get a hold on you."

"Nobody has a hold on me, Dad."

"Not yet. But one thought leads to another. Before you know it, you'll be exploring all sorts of ideas together, knowing each other so well you'll finish each other's sentences."

"Okay," I said. "Okay."

"Stick to lovemaking."

"Right," I said.

"Don't discuss ideas."

"Dad," I said, "kids today—"

"Not nice kids. Aren't you a nice kid?"

"Yeah, I'm a nice kid."

"And Eleanor, too?"

"Yeah, Eleanor, too."

"Then show some respect for her. Don't ask her opinions. I know it's you who starts it."

"Okay," I said.

"Okay?" he said. He mussed up my hair, gave me a poke in the ribs, and went down to breakfast.

By the time I got downstairs, he'd finished his eggs and was sipping coffee, holding hands with my mother.

I don't think they've exchanged an idea in years.

To tell you the truth, I can't imagine them exchanging ideas, ever, though I know they did. She has a collection of letters he wrote to her on every subject from Shakespeare to Bach, and he treasures this little essay she wrote for him when they were engaged, on her feelings about French drama.

All I've ever seen them do is hug and kiss. Maybe they wait until I'm asleep to get into their discussions. Who knows?

I walked to school with Edna O'Leary.

She's very beautiful. I'll say that for her. We put our arms around each other, held tight, and stopped to kiss along the way. But I'd never ask her opinion on any subject. She just doesn't appeal to me that way.

"I love your eyes, John," she said.

"I love your smile, Edna."

"Do you like this color on me?"

"I like you in blue better."

"Oh, John, that's interesting, because I like you in blue, too."

We chatted and kissed and laughed as we went up the winding walk to school.

In the schoolyard everyone was cuddled up except for some of the lovers, who were off walking in pairs, talking. I doubted that they were saying trivial things. Their fingers were pointing and their hands were moving, and they were frowning.

You can always tell the ones in love by their passionate gestures as they get into conversations.

I went into the Boys' room for a smoke.

That's right, I'm starting to smoke. That's the state of mind I'm in.

My father says I'm going through a typical teen-age stage, but I don't think he understands how crazy it's making me. He says he went through the same thing, but I just can't picture that.

On the bathroom wall there were heads drawn with kids' initials inside.

There was the usual graffiti:

Josephine Merril is a brain! I'd like to know her opinions!

If you'd like some interesting conversation, try Loulou.

I smoked a cigarette and thought of Lauren Lake.

Who didn't think of Lauren? I made a bet with myself that there were half a dozen guys like me remembering Lauren's answer to Mr. Porter's question last week in Thoughts class.

A few more answers like that, and those parents who want Thoughts taken out of the school curriculum will have their way. Some kid will run home and tell the folks what goes on in Porter's room, and Thoughts will be replaced by another course in history, language, body maintenance, sex education, or some other boring subject that isn't supposed to be provocative.

"What are dreams?" Mr. Porter asked.

Naturally, Lauren's hand shot up first. She can't help herself.

"Lauren?"

"Dreams can be waking thoughts or sleeping thoughts," she said. "I had a dream once, a waking one, about a world where you could say anything on your mind, but you had to be very careful about who you touched. You could ask anyone his opinion, but you couldn't just go up and kiss him."

Some of the kids got red-faced and sucked in their breaths. Even Porter said, "Now, take it easy, Lauren. Some of your classmates aren't as advanced as you are."

One kid yelled out, "If you had to be careful about touching, how would you reproduce in that world?"

"The same way we do in our world," Lauren said, "only lovemaking would be a special thing. It would be the intimate thing, and discussing ideas would be a natural thing."

"That's a good way to cheapen the exchange of ideas!" someone muttered.

Everyone was laughing and nudging the ones next to them, but my mind was spinning. I bet other kids were about to go out of their minds, too.

Mr. Porter ran back and kissed Lauren.

She couldn't seem to stop.

She said, "What's wrong with a free exchange of ideas?"

"Ideas are personal," someone said. "Bodies are all alike, but ideas are individual and personal."

Mr. Porter held Lauren's hand. "Keep it to yourself, Lauren," he said. "Just keep it to yourself."

"In my opinion," Lauren began, but Mr. Porter had to get her under control, so he just pressed his mouth against hers until she was quiet.

"Don't tell *everything* you're thinking, darling," he warned her. "I know this is a class on thoughts, but we have to have *some* modesty."

Lauren just can't quit. She's a brain, and that mind of

hers is going to wander all over the place. It just is. She's that kind of girl.

Sometimes I think I'm that kind of boy, and not the nice boy I claim to be. Do you know what I mean? I want to tell someone what I think about the books I read, not just recite the plots. And I want to ask someone what she thinks about World War II, not just go over its history. And I want to . . .

Nevermind.

Listen—the heck with it!

It's not what's up there that counts.

Love makes the world go round. Lovemaking is what's important—relaxing your body, letting your mind empty —just feeling without thinking—just giving in and letting go.

There'll be time enough to exchange ideas, make points —all of it. I'll meet the right girl someday and we'll have the rest of our lives to confide in each other.

"Class come to order!" Mr. Porter finally got Lauren quieted down. "Now, a dream is a succession of images or ideas present in the mind mainly during sleep. It is an involuntary vision . . ."

On and on, while we all reached for each other's hands, gave each other kisses, and got back to normal.

I put that memory out of my poor messed-up mind, and put out my cigarette.

I was ready to face another day, and I told myself, Hey, you're going to be okay. Tonight, you'll get Dad's car, get a date with someone like Edna O'Leary, go off someplace and whisper loving things into her ear, and feel her soft long blond hair tickle your face, tell her you love her, tell her she's beautiful . . .

I swung through the door of the Boys' room, and headed down the hall, whistling, walking fast.

Then I saw Lauren, headed right toward me.

She looked carefully at me, and I looked carefully at her.

She frowned a little. I frowned a lot.

I did everything to keep from blurting out, "Lauren, what do you think about outer space travel?" . . . "Lauren, what do you think of Kurt Vonnegut's writing?" . . . "Lauren, do you think the old Beatles' music is profound or shallow?"

For a moment my mind went blank while we stood without smiling or touching.

Then she kissed my lips, and I slid my arm around her waist.

"Hi, John, dear!" She grinned.

"Hi, Lauren, sweetheart!" I grinned back.

I almost said, "Would you like to go out tonight?" But it isn't fair to ask a girl out when all you really want is one thing.

I held her very close to me and gently told her that her hair smelled like the sun, and her lips tasted as sweet as red summer apples. Yet all the while I was thinking, Oh, Lauren, we're making a mistake with China, in my opinion. . . . Oh, Lauren, Lauren, from your point of view, how do things look in the Middle East?

M. E. KERR

M. E. Kerr was born Marijane Meaker in Auburn, New York, and is now a resident of East Hampton on Long Island. She attended the University of Missouri and then moved to New York City, where she published her first story in the *Ladies' Home Journal* in 1951.

Her earliest and best-known novel, *Dinky Hocker Shoots Smack!* is about an overweight girl who "overdoses" on food to compensate for the lack of attention from her parents. In addition to being named a Best Children's Book of 1972 by *School Library Journal,* it was made into an ABC-TV Afterschool Special.

Many of her novels—*The Son of Someone Famous; If I Love You, Am I Trapped Forever?; Is That You, Miss Blue?;* and, more recently, *What I Really Think of You*—have more intricate plots and are peopled by more unusual characters than those found in most other young adult novels. Her most unusual character is a beautiful seventeen-year-old female, the title character in *Little Little,* who is only three feet three inches tall and is in love with Sydney Cinnamon, another little person who plays "The Roach" in a TV pest-control commercial.

Although it begins as a summer romance between two mismatched teen-agers, *Gentlehands*—perhaps Kerr's most sophisticated novel for young adults—slowly unfolds as a hunt for an ex-Nazi war criminal.

In addition to Ms. Kerr's award-winning novels for teen-agers, as M. J. Meaker she has written books for adults and has published adult mysteries under the name of Vin Packer. M. E. Kerr's own zany teen-age adventures and the models for some of her adolescent characters are described in her recent autobiography, *Me Me Me Me Me, Not a Novel.*

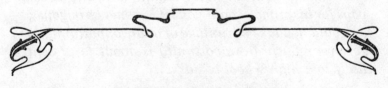

DECISIONS

A former "friend" steals a substantial amount of money from you but never admits to it and never pays for his crime. Would you let bygones be bygones, or would you take advantage of a rare opportunity to get even? Such an opportunity is about to present itself to a high school senior. . . .

FOURTH OF JULY

ROBIN F. BRANCATO

Chuck draws the squeegee carefully across the windshield and lets it sink back into the bucket of water at his feet. "Check the oil, sir?" he asks.

"No, thanks."

"That'll be fifteen dollars even, then."

The customer hands him the money and starts up the engine.

"Happy Fourth of July," Chuck calls, standing there for a moment, stretching the muscles of his arms, as the car pulls away from the pump. Nice night, he thinks. Crickets singing behind the station. Drum and bugle corps warming up in the distance. Kids setting off caps somewhere down the street. Seventy-four degrees, Chuck sees by the thermometer mounted on the side of the oilcan rack. Warm enough for a midnight dip in Kate's pool maybe, after the fireworks. If he gets out of here on time, that is.

"Chuck?"

"Coming." He turns toward the white tile building—the station where he's worked for two summers now. Could be worse, he decides, glancing up at the TUNE UP HERE sign and at the red, white, and blue banners flapping over his head. He could be filing papers in an office,

or have no job at all. Next summer, with high school behind him, he'll try for something else.

"Chuck?"

He can see Kate, sitting on the desk in the office part of
the station, her profile so excellent in the neon glow.
Freshly washed hair, pushed back behind her ears. Graceful, like a dancer, especially compared to Bobby-the-Hulk,
who's tilting back on the station's one beat-up chair.

"Think we should go on, Chuck?" Kate is framed in the
doorway now. "Should Bobby and I pick up Eileen and
get a good place to sit, and you'll meet us later?"

Chuck pauses just outside the door, by the potted gera-
niums. "Yeah, you'd better, in a couple of minutes," he
says reluctantly. "I can't get out of here until ten at the
earliest." Squeezing Kate's arm as he passes, he opens the
cash register and puts in the bills. "Vic *said* something,
you know, the last time he came by and saw I had com-
pany."

"Said something?" Bobby rocks forward heavily. "You
mean Big Boss Victor gave you flak because of us?"

Chuck closes the register. "Says he doesn't want the
place to look like a hangout." He smiles. "Don't worry. All
you have to do is get off your butt and buy a quart of oil if
he comes around."

"I couldn't if I wanted to." Bobby sticks his hands in the
pockets of his painter's pants. "Spent my last couple of
bucks until payday on these." With a flourish he pulls out
several little red cylinders and holds them up by their
fuses. "M-80s. I got more in my car. Bottle rockets, too,
and some other junk. I'm putting on my own show when
the firemen finish theirs tonight."

"Oh, but the fireworks in the park are so nice," Kate
says. "*Those* things . . ." She makes a face.

"Where'd you get 'em?" Chuck asks.

Bobby's chair creaks. "My sister's boyfriend brought
them up from down South. The best you can get. Each
M-80 equals one-fifth stick of dynamite." He looks at
Chuck. "Want to go halves with me?"

"Nope, I got better things to do with my money."

Bobby, rocking back and forth, balances the M-80s on his stomach. "You mean you're hurting as bad as I am?"

"Let's say she's making me watch the bucks." Straightening the pile of road maps by the register, Chuck nods toward Kate. "She's being a good influence, you know?"

"Sounds pretty boring to me. Did she get you to quit smoking yet?"

"Not yet. In the fall I'm going to quit."

Bobby, sighing, makes the firecrackers dance on his stomach. "What are you guys saving up for—*a down payment on a house?*"

Kate's laugh rings out.

"Hell, no, man." Chuck smiles. "I'm still thinking cars. *You* put a car first until you got one—you should know."

"How much more do you need?"

"A lot. What did I figure yesterday, Kate? Another five hundred?"

"About that."

Bobby, picking up the M-80s by their fuses, rotates them gently. "Five hundred's a lot." He glances up. "Think you'll ever get back what Sager took from you?"

Chuck turns abruptly. "Don't even bring that up, okay? I go crazy when I hear his name. *No.* I told you before, I'm not getting anything back. The judge invited Sager to court and slapped his hands, that's all."

"I don't get it." Bobby shifts in the chair. "Can't they make Sager's mother pay?"

"I don't know if they can, but the point is, they *didn't.*" Chuck glances out as a car takes a shortcut through the station. "I did all I could," he goes on. "Kate'll tell you how much time it took. When I heard Sager was finally going to court a couple of months ago, I wrote a letter to the judge."

"It was a really good letter," Kate says.

"What'd you say?" Bobby slips the M-80s under his T-shirt.

"Hell, I told him the whole story. 'Dear Judge.' " Chuck

cracks his knuckles. " 'This is about something that happened to me almost a year ago. How would *you* feel if a guy on your street that you never liked but always tried to be decent to, came over to your house one night when you were home alone, and you're rapping with him, and you mention you just got your last two weeks' pay, and while you're getting him a Coke he sneaks up to your bedroom and helps himself to your two hundred bucks?' "

A chair spoke pops as Bobby sits up. "The judge knew Sager did it, right? He knew the cops got his fingerprints off your bureau?"

"Everybody knows Sager did it," Chuck says. "They've had his prints on file for three years. They had him in court that day on five other charges besides mine!"

"What'd you want the judge to do with him?"

"Have him make restitution. 'The only way I'll be satisfied,' I told the judge, 'is if the court makes him pay me back—me and the other people he stole from.' "

"No dice, though, huh?" Bobby sniffs. "Some judge."

Chuck feels himself heating up. "Yeah, losing two hundred bucks is nothing to those guys."

"Wait a second." Kate's hand is on his arm. "That's probably not true. Maybe the judge thinks giving him one more chance will straighten him out. You know what they say about prisons, how awful they are."

"Oh, man, not *this* again!" Chuck snaps his eyes shut. "Poor Sager, his father died when he was a kid, so we got to let him get away with everything! Come off it, Kate." He walks away from her, toward the tire rack. "Lots of guys have no father, and they don't all become crooks— crooks who specialize in ripping off *friends.*" Chuck bangs his elbow against the rack. "What the hell, what do *you* know? If you were a guy you'd understand."

Kate shakes her head wearily. "That has nothing to do with it. I can't stand Jack Sager, you know that. And I know how you worked for that money." She gathers her hair up in one hand. "It's just that—I don't think it's so

dumb to think that people can change. *You've* changed
since I met you. You're much saner. Isn't that true?"

Chuck yanks at his T-shirt. "Yes . . . *no!* Who's talking
about me, anyway?"

"Oh, boy," Bobby snorts. "Better watch yourself, man.
Stick with this chick and you'll get to be pope—Pope
Chuck the First. Listen," he says, rising from the chair, "I
got one thing to tell you, and then her and me'll get
moving. I saw Sager today. He's back in town from wher-
ever his mother shipped him off to."

Kate rolls her eyes.

"Where?" Chuck asks. "Where'd you see him?"

"Cruising the park this afternoon. In a practically new
green Buick."

"His?"

"He said it was. Who knows?"

"You talked to him?"

"A little. Not about your money."

"He denies it," Chuck says angrily. "He swore to the
cops that his fingerprints were in my room because I took
him up there to smoke a joint!"

Bobby slaps the cigarette machine. "Look, you want
advice? Forget the judge. Even things up on your own,
man. Punch him out if you see him, or slit his tires. Rip off
two hundred bucks' worth of stuff from his old lady. She's
not poor."

Kate groans.

Bobby, pulling car keys from his pocket, nudges her
playfully. "Just kidding, Katie. Katie doesn't go for that
stuff. Come on, let's pick up Eileen."

Kate pauses in the doorway as Bobby squeezes past her.
"Chuck?"

"Yeah?" He loves her hair in the yellow neon light. He
loves that serious expression of hers.

"You'll stay away from Jack, won't you?"

"Do I look like I'm about to get up a posse?"

Kate, inching closer, reaches for his hand. "I mean, if
you see him at the park or somewhere, you won't get

involved with him? Don't think about the money, Chuck. You're doing so well—"

"The money's only part of it."

"I know, but *avoid* him—promise?"

Pulling her toward him, he feels her softness and strength.

"You don't have to prove anything," Kate says.

"Don't *worry.*" He lets his hands slide down her arms. "Where'll I see you—on the hill where we sat last time?"

She nods. "I brought a blanket. It's a long walk to the park from here. I hope you get there before it's over."

"I'll make it as soon as I can." Hugging her again, he kisses her hard.

"Hey!" Bobby, by the pumps, pounds on a five-gallon can. "This isn't good-bye forever, you guys. Come on, Katie, time's up!"

Chuck watches them cross the lot and climb into Bobby's Chevy. "See you later," he calls as they drive away. Then, drifting back to the office, he lights a cigarette with his Bic. Slow night. Might as well start cleaning up the place. He stoops to pick up a paper cup, a gum wrapper— what's that thing? Stamping out his cigarette, he scoops up the red cylinder, one of Bobby's stray toys. Then, distracted by a customer driving up to the island, he drops the M-80 into his pocket. "Evening, sir," he says. "Would you like me to fill it up?"

Chuck glances at the clock. Two minutes to ten. He hears the far-off *boom* of drums now. There's a low whistling sound, too, and when he looks up he sees an orange burst. They've started the aerial fireworks. As soon as he closes up, he can take off for the park. First, haul down the green flag and lock up the oilcan rack. Don't trip over the water bucket. Bring in the credit card machine. Open the safe and put in the cash. Make sure the safe is closed tight. What else? Fix the spoke on the broken chair, so Vic won't take a fit.

Getting a pad and pencil from the desk drawer, Chuck

goes out and records the final readings on the pumps. A long, low whistle sounds again. He watches with pleasure as a tiny orange ball rises and explodes into a flower in the sky. Snakelike things wriggle from its center, and Chuck is so caught up that he isn't aware of the green Buick until it comes to a stop on the near side of the pump.

The sound of rock radio pours through the car's open windows. Chuck feels his whole body clenching.

"Hey!" Jack Sager's long, narrow face is eerie in the fluorescent light.

Chuck, clearing his throat, doesn't move.

"Still on the job, huh?" Sager, a faint smile on his lips, turns off the engine and adjusts his handkerchief headband. "How's it going?"

The core of heat rising in Chuck lodges in his throat.

Sager dangles one sinewy arm out the window. A shock of straight dark hair, free of the headband, falls in his eyes. "You open for business or what?"

"Closing," Chuck says. He clears his throat again.

"But not actually *closed,* right? Give me eight bucks' worth." Sager digs into his pocket.

Chuck still doesn't move. A chain of memories set off by Sager's grin fixes him to the spot: Sager handing him a soapsuds milkshake; Sager forging his name on a dirty note to a girl; Sager looking over his shoulder in the biology exam . . . All of this he shrugged off because Sager was just kidding around, right? Or else—Chuck feels himself sweating—or else because of fear that the guy, when crossed, might do even worse. How come whenever his parents warned him about Sager he'd get mad, not at Sager but at *them?* No more letting things go by. "I'm closed," Chuck says. "I already wrote down the totals."

"Hey, have a heart." Sager's face bursts into a smile. "I'm running on empty," he says. "You know that song?"

"Yeah," Chuck answers. "Walk home and stick it up your tape deck."

Sager laughs. "I'm not kidding around, man. I glided in here on my last drop."

"Good. Sit here all night."

Sager, his smile fading, opens the car door and sets one foot on the ground. "What's the problem? You still think I took your money?"

"I know you did." Sweat is trickling down Chuck's armpits.

Sager shakes his head. "You got a overactive imagination," he says, "you and the cops, both. You're lucky they didn't find your stash in your bureau that night."

Chuck clenches his hands. "Your crooked lawyer's the only one who'd believe that ridiculous story."

Sager's other foot drops to the ground. "Give me the gas, man, or I help myself. You don't want to be eight bucks short, do you?"

Chuck's eyes dart from Sager's face to the five-gallon can by the pump. Eight bucks' worth. He lifts the can—it's empty. Go ahead, why not? Steadying his voice, he says, "Cool it, Sager. I'll give it to you. Get in your car and fork over the money. See the sign? 'Exact change after nine P.M.' *Up front,* that means."

"What's the matter," Sager smirks, "you guys don't trust your customers?" Sitting back in the seat, he pulls out a five and three ones.

Chuck stuffs the money in his pocket. Then as Sager slams the car door and starts fiddling with the radio, Chuck lifts the hose off the pump. Heavy-metal rock drifts through the open windows of the Buick. Partly hidden by the pump, Chuck keeps both eyes on Sager. In his right hand is the hose. In his left, the empty can. Letting the gas flow, Chuck catches it in the can that is on the ground under the tank. Perfect.

Sager glances over his shoulder at the pump's spinning numbers, then turns up the radio and slouches in the seat, his head resting on the seatback. Numbers spin—two dollars, three dollars, four—

Sager is singing along with the radio now, tapping rhythms on the wheel. Chuck stares in fascination as the gas level rises in the can. When it reaches the top, he puts the hose on the ground and lets a little more run out. And when the meter reads $8.00, he cuts the flow and puts the hose back on the pump. "Okay, Sager, get going."

Sager doesn't hear him at first because the music is so loud. Chuck stands there with his hands in his pockets. "I'm in a hurry, get going!"

The *thump-thump* of the radio fades and Sager's head pops out the window. "Trying to get rid of me? What kind of a attitude is that?"

Chuck, glaring in the window, feels his fingers touch something in his pocket.

Sager grins. "Still holding a grudge, huh? How do you know one of your other friends didn't rip you off?"

Chuck's hand closes over the fuse, the cardboard shell.

"Maybe Bobby," Sager insists. "He needed money to buy his car then."

Chuck's other hand touches his lighter.

Sager turns up the radio again. "Why not let bygones be bygones, man? I'm going back to Texas tomorrow for good. Did you say you were in a hurry? How about if I drop you somewhere?"

"Okay," Chuck says hoarsely. His heart pounds along with the radio. "Wait'll I—shut these off."

Easing behind the pumps, he flicks his lighter and a bright flame leaps upward. He draws the cylinder toward it, but the fuse doesn't catch. His hands are shaking so bad that the M-80 wobbles. His ears are ringing, as if people are shouting at him. Try again! And make it quick, before Sager notices the gas gauge still on empty. He flicks again. This time the fuse catches and a red flame creeps down.

In a daze Chuck sweeps around the car, almost tripping over the water bucket. He measures the distance to the open back window of the Buick, knowing he'll never get another chance like this. Throw it!

"What's taking so long?"

Chuck juggles the thing in one hand. Gas fumes are floating up—get rid of it! Gas is trickling toward him from under the car. The fuse is almost gone. Get rid of it now!

He does. With a sudden whirling motion he tosses it into the bucket of water by the pump. Do they explode in water? Please, *no.*

"Y'almost ready?" Sager calls.

Chuck's eyes are shut. When he opens them, the bucket is still there. He stares at it to make sure. "Go on without me, Sager," he says hoarsely, stepping out from behind the pumps. "I just remembered my dad's picking me up."

"Yeah? When?"

"Any minute. This'll be him, probably." Shielding his eyes, he nods at a car stopping for the light on the corner.

"Your old man?"

"Yeah, it should be. See you around, Sager," Chuck says.

Sager, looking over his shoulder, revs the engine noisily. "Tell him hello from me." He smirks as the car bucks forward.

"I will," Chuck says, slapping the Buick as if to push it off.

Sager leans out the window. "Hope you catch the right guy one of these days!" Burning rubber, he digs out.

Chuck watches the Buick's taillights fade. As the car that has been waiting at the light starts up and goes on, Chuck quickly empties the water bucket in the bushes, puts the eight dollars in the safe, turns off the lights, and locks the station door. Then, with the rumble of fireworks in his ears, he jogs to meet Kate, taking surprisingly little satisfaction from the thought that very soon Sager may be stalled out on a dark, lonely road.

ROBIN FIDLER BRANCATO

After teaching English to high school students in Hackensack, New Jersey, and raising two adolescents of her own, Robin Brancato knows teen-agers. Perhaps that's partly why her young adult novels have been so well liked.

Although her first novel, *Don't Sit Under the Apple Tree,* did not get a lot of attention, her second one did. *Something Left to Lose* is the story of the close friendship of three girls and their interest in astrology. That book was followed by the even more successful *Winning,* the story of a star football player's sudden injury and how a sensitive English teacher helps him learn to cope and to accept his paralyzed condition. In 1977 the American Library Association named *Winning* a Best Book for Young Adults.

That same honor was bestowed on two of Ms. Brancato's later novels for teen-agers: *Come Alive at 505* and *Sweet Bells Jangled Out of Tune.* Her third novel, *Blinded by the Light,* an examination of the effects of a religious cult on its members and on one family in particular, was made into a CBS Movie of the Week starring Kristy McNichol.

Raised in Wyomissing, Pennsylvania, and educated at the University of Pennsylvania and the City College of New York, Robin Brancato now lives in Teaneck, New Jersey, with her husband, John, and their two sons. Her newest young adult novel is *Facing Up.*

Some kids have always taken a special interest in finding ways to drive teachers crazy. Some students, of course, see the teacher as "the enemy," never thinking about how the teacher feels. Seldom does the teacher get to tell his side of the story. . . .

THREE PEOPLE AND TWO SEATS

KEVIN MAJOR

Outside the garage the air was chilled and the evening dark except for the light from the gas pumps. It revealed scattered specks of falling snow that would otherwise have been invisible. They touched the ground lightly, hesitated, then disappeared. Beyond the garage and out to the highway the darkness expanded wider and blacker, completely unbroken.

"That bloody thing will never get here," he turned and said to the guy who had sold him the ticket. "It's a half-hour late already."

The fellow, held in the spell of the comic he was reading, didn't bother to look up. He nodded slightly and mumbled in agreement.

"Damn bus. Never on time." He turned and stared out the window again. He stood there forcing his hands tighter into his gloves, the fingers of one hand pressing against the spaces between the fingers of the other. Then, just for a moment, he thought it might be the bus coming. It wasn't—the headlights were too low, not powerful enough.

The car's horn demanding gas finally disturbed the attendant's concentration. He brought the chair he was sitting on back to its legs and himself slowly to his feet. Spider-Man was carefully laid aside.

"You'll just have to wait I guess," the fellow said on his
way through the door.

"Wait?" . . . How much longer? Come Tuesday morning he would have to be back to start work again.

This long weekend break would allow him momentary
recovery from the strain of the previous two months. It
had been a hard decline from the eagerness and confidence that he had arrived with at this same bus stop in
September.

The bus showed up eventually. He left the inside of the
garage when he saw the lights round the highway curve.
Its engine roaring, it geared down and stopped almost
directly opposite where he stood. He grabbed his overnight bag and climbed the three steps. The driver took his
ticket.

"You'll have to stand. All the seats are taken," the driver
told him as he punched two precise holes.

He made no reply but walked with his case toward the
rear of the bus. Dim, floor-level lights marked the way. As
he walked he checked all the seats. Every one was filled—
by curled, motionless bodies—by those who opened their
eyes long enough to mutter, "How far are we now?"—the
others by half-smiling, comfortable faces.

As the bus returned to the highway, he was in the back,
the sole person standing, supporting himself with the
handrail that ran beneath the luggage rack. He pushed his
case up among the other bags and leaned back against the
washroom cubicle. Then he cursed under his breath.
Standing. Grand Falls was over fifty miles away. At least
an hour before there would be a chance of a vacant seat.

"You might be able to squeeze in here." The voice was
friendly, though weak and unsure.

He did not reply right away, but turned and saw two
boys. It was only then he was certain he was being spoken
to.

"There's not much room. We can move over."

"Thanks."

They were the farthest back of the seats on the bus, just behind where he had been standing and left of the washroom door. It definitely beat standing up. He sat down as the third person in a space normally occupied by two people. Because the others were small, the fit was a tight one but not uncomfortable.

"Where you headed for?"

The two boys were more anxious than he was to exchange questions. He would have been content to remain silent and let them continue as they were before he sat down. They had given him a seat; he couldn't ignore that.

"Gander."

His reply left an unexpected silence. He could feel they were waiting for more than one word.

"What about you fellows?"

"Bishops Falls. That's where Kenny's aunt is. We don't live there, just goin' for a visit." The kid brushed the hair away from his eyes and scratched the back of his neck in one motion. "We've been there lots of times before."

The interior of the bus was obscure for the most part. Here and there reading lights provided small measures of illumination. The one above the seat ahead revealed that the fellow who had been speaking was the shorter of the two boys, despite the fact that he looked older, probably fourteen. He had a dark complexion and black hair, which kept falling forward into his eyes. A quick smile revealed his potential for mischief. His buddy, next to the window, was blond with hair that curled above the edge of his baseball cap. He seemed to be the quieter but equal partner.

"My name is Brian. And that's Kenny." They were words that hung loose. Again they waited for him to answer.

He knew there was no good reason not to. "Mine is Dave."

The boys were eased. "You want a smoke, Dave?"

"No thanks."

"You sure? We bought a pack between us this mornin'."

He brought to view from the inside reaches of his shirt a package of cigarettes and made an offer with the opened end.

"No thanks. I don't smoke much."

"We could save you a draw."

Each of the boys put one in his mouth. Brian returned the pack to its former location and pulled out some matches from his pants pocket. As they lit up, Dave could see they were seasoned smokers. It wasn't boyish misbehavior with them any longer. They blew smoke rings into the light above the next seat and watched them float away, out of shape.

"Geez," Brian whispered to his friend after they'd been sitting quietly for only a minute, "we could have that guy up there smoked out in no time. He'd have to throw away his book and come up for air."

"Go for it."

"Sure."

"Go on."

"You."

Kenny took a deep draw on his cigarette, then burst out with fake sputtering coughs.

"Cut it out, jerk!" Brian warned him in a heavy, lowered voice. "You're gettin' ashes all over me."

A fist banged against Kenny's leg.

"Oow!" The sound rose sharply.

There was a brief silence, then a revenge hit from Kenny.

It didn't produce a great deal of noise overall. It didn't seem to be bothering anyone, Dave noticed, and it wasn't bothering him. He had grown up through that kind of behavior too . . . though maybe he had not been so boisterous. They were kids having fun. Perhaps, he thought, it should be annoying him.

But a bus ride and a classroom are two different situations. Sitting there, he suddenly realized that. At the beginning of September he never would have accepted such an idea. He might even have considered it to be out-moded thinking.

Kenny poked his friend. "As Rabbit would say, 'You have no manners.' "

"No she don't. It's 'Brian, you have absolutely no manners!' " he mimicked, his voice highly pitched. Then low-ered, "I could teach her a few things."

There followed lewd mumblings interspersed with whistles.

"Absolutely no manners."

"Boys, you're a hard bunch," he said to them, shaking his head with the hint of a smile. He couldn't sit and listen any longer without making some comment.

"Nah."

"Your aunt doesn't know what she's in for. She expect-ing you?"

"Probably," Kenny said. "I go over there almost every holiday we get. She won't be surprised."

He felt there would be a flood of conversation if he gave them the opportunity. Kenny made a motion to him with the filter end of his lighted cigarette. He refused again.

"It's better than being in Corner Brook I'll tell ya."

"You might say. Nothin' for us to do there but hang around the sidewalks. Or get kicked outa restaurants for not buyin' anything."

Brian drew back his head sternly. "Kids your age—"

"Hey, Brian, where's those sandwiches your mother gave you before you left?"

"Probably lost by now."

"Get 'em. I'm starved. You hungry, Dave?"

Brian stretched out and moved his hand across on the luggage rack until it struck upon a brown paper bag. Opening it, he withdrew a can of Pepsi and a small stack of sandwiches wrapped in wax paper. They consisted of thin slices of bologna between pieces of buttered bread.

"Do you want one?" he offered their guest. "There's nothin' wrong with 'em, honest."

The food stared up uninvitingly. "Okay." When he held

it in his hand, it slid apart. "Your mother makes a slippery sandwich." They laughed.

"She was glad enough to see me go," Brian said, as if it were part of the humor.

How could he react to that? The kid regretted having said it and dug his buddy with an elbow.

"Jerk, gimme a drink o' Pepsi." He drank and sucked the can until it was dry.

"You didn't have to drink it all. At least you could have saved me a mouthful."

"Here's the can."

"I don't want an empty can." They juggled it back and forth, and it fell to the floor with a clamor.

The too loud noise put a quick lid on their antics. They returned to the sandwiches.

Had he been sitting in another seat, he would probably have been asleep by now, like most of the other passengers. But instead he was consuming the last bit of a stale sandwich next to a pair of disquieting boys. They gave him a great deal to think about. He couldn't help but picture the boys' homes left behind in Corner Brook. Their exteriors were real enough; he had passed enough of them to know how they looked. What took place inside he had gathered from a mixture of his sociology readings, of movies and novels, and the rough kids at school.

The picture stirred him. They would be forced to grow serious in time, he thought. Then the fun would be gone.

"We should be getting pretty close to Grand Falls by now," he said after a long silence.

Kenny peered through the window. "Can't see nothin' yet."

"You wouldn't see much anyway until we're just about there," he said, yawning.

"Why don't you take a nap? We'll keep quiet. I'll make Kenny shut up if I have to stuff his mouth—"

"Listen who's talkin'," his friend cut in.

"Never mind. It won't be much longer." He yawned a second time. "You fellows don't look very sleepy."

"Nah. Takes the fun outa goin' anywhere if you sleep all the time."

He recalled occasions when he would have said the same thing.

The stop at Grand Falls gave him a chance to stretch his legs. He left the bus without a coat and the cold night air abruptly cleared his head of any sleepiness. He went inside the restaurant and waited in front of the lunch counter.

Within a few minutes he reentered the bus, shivering, holding three small cardboard plates of French fries, each topped with a plastic fork and a packet of ketchup.

"Perhaps you're still a bit hungry."

They looked awkward accepting it. He thought that perhaps it was because they weren't very often in such a position.

"That's all right. Go ahead, take it. Except for you guys I would still be standing up."

They repeated their thanks a number of times. It seemed out of proportion to what he had given them.

"That's okay, I won't go broke because of it." They ate quietly now, but with obvious pleasure.

It reminded him of the time, about a year before, he had been hitchhiking home from university. He hadn't bothered to stop anywhere all day to eat, but stayed on the road to make it home before dark. Then, late in the evening, with thirty miles still remaining, a bakery van picked him up. The driver gave him a free hand with the leftovers in the back. He stuffed himself on apple turnovers and chocolate-covered doughnuts. At that time, a thank-you seemed inadequate.

"Good, eh?"

"Yeah."

"I can never eat French fries with a fork," he said to them. "Only with my fingers."

The door at the front closed. The driver switched off the

center overhead lights and headed the bus back on the highway.

"You fellows finished? Here, put the plates in this bag. Don't want the floor littered up."

The next thing they did, almost as if it were an automatic reaction, was to get out their cigarettes. He refused on the first offer.

"You sure? Com'on, have one." It was to be a return gift. Kenny held out the pack.

"Okay. You convinced me."

"Brian, get your matches out again."

Brian dug them from his pocket and lit the three cigarettes. He waved out the match and found the bag to put it in. It was like a relaxing after-dinner smoke.

"What do you do? I mean . . . do you work?" one of them asked.

"Yeah." He hesitated. "I'm a schoolteacher."

They looked at each other quickly and smiled, then looked back in anticipation of him laughing.

"You're not a teacher."

He was sorry now that he had said it. He wished he had sidestepped the question. "Okay, I'm not."

"Then what do you do?"

He removed his wallet from a coat pocket and produced a white card for them to read.

"Here, read this. What does it say?"

"Newfoundland Teachers—"

"Association. And it has my name on it."

"You could have made that up yourself."

He shook his head.

"All right then, what grade do you teach?"

"Eight, most of the time."

"Kenny, you think he's tellin' the truth?" They figured he might be trying to pull a fast one on them.

"There are thousands of teachers, you know. Why is that so hard to believe?"

"You don't look like one. Besides, I've never seen a

teacher like you, eh, Kenny? Every one of the teachers at our school are crabs, except maybe for Mrs. Lewis."

"And she don't even teach us."

Perhaps he should have felt flattered, but suddenly lurking back to deaden any contentment was the thought of the experiences of the past weeks.

"Tell me now, what would you boys do if you had me for a teacher?"

"Guess we could have a bit of fun."

It wasn't what he had hoped for. Neither was it a surprise.

"Maybe you would learn something."

"Nah, not me."

"Me neither."

"Couldn't beat anything into my head."

Damnit! He should have known better than to ask. What was he expecting?

"You wouldn't want to be a teacher very long in our school anyway. There was a guy there last year only lasted two weeks. We almost drove him crazy." They were laughing.

"Was he tough on you?"

"Nah, we almost took right over. He was an okay guy, I mean he would have been all right, but he never could keep order."

"You could have given him a chance! Sure, perhaps he was trying to help you guys."

"We were only havin' a bit o' fun. He couldn't even get real mad with us."

"That all you wanted to do—make him mad! You think I wouldn't last two weeks?"

"Wha'?"

"You think I wouldn't last two weeks!" he repeated forcefully. "You think I'd crack up too?"

What kind of fool was he anyway? Trying to be reasonable with kids. He turned from them.

He must be some kind of damned idiot. They were right

—cracked in two weeks. Face it—two weeks, two months, it was all the same.

As a teacher he was nothing! He liked kids, didn't he? And hadn't he tried to show that? Or did that matter? Did he have to pretend to hate them before they would behave in the classroom? Did he have to play Jekyll and Hyde?

He recalled when he went into his first class—he was nervous but his intentions were good. He knew what he wanted to do. He wanted response to what he was teaching. He wanted their opinions. Not facts. Feelings. On an equal basis.

He read somewhere later that any teacher who smiles very much before the end of six weeks is inviting trouble. Too bad. He wasn't going to take any advice from what must have been some sour spinster.

He couldn't deny now though that he had been creamed. From then on, whenever he wanted seriousness, it was hell to get it. He had reasoned wrongly. Show them that you know real life is not all easy, show them that you understand—they will respond then; they'll make an honest try. Like hell. They didn't see it that way. For most of them it meant he was a soft teacher. Someone to take advantage of. Someone who didn't even send people to the principal.

They just couldn't understand a teacher who didn't jump on them. That's the way it's played—the guy up front yells; they sit and stay quiet.

"Sorry, we didn't mean it that way." Brian spoke shyly.

His mind reverted to them quietly sitting there. They looked at him awkwardly. He knew he would remember it later as one of those times when he wished he had said something else, but didn't.

Damnit, he wanted to get this straight!

They left the bus at Bishops Falls, the next stop. He couldn't come up with much to say even then. He smiled at them from inside as they headed down the road. That was the only way he could put it.

He was now one person with two seats. The one beside him remained vacant for the rest of the trip. It was a luxury, almost a bed if he wanted to sleep. He never gave a second thought to using it. He buttoned up his coat and put on his gloves. He sat there, hardly stirring then for the next hour, until the bus stopped at Gander. He got off, leaving the two seats unoccupied, except for the four torn pieces of a white card.

KEVIN MAJOR

Although he won four major book awards in Canada for his first young adult novel, Kevin Major has only recently begun to get the attention he deserves in the United States. The youngest of seven children of a Newfoundland fisherman, Kevin Major grew up in the town of Stephenville. After planning to be a physician, he eventually decided to become a teacher. While teaching seventh- and eighth-grade science and English in the small town of Robert's Arm, he developed an interest in writing—especially about his homeland.

His first book—*Doryloads*—is a collection of stories and poems about the unique culture and heritage of Newfoundland and is illustrated with Kevin's own photographs. Pleased with the success of that book, he quit teaching—though he continues to substitute in Eastport—and wrote his first novel. *Hold Fast* is the story of a courageous teenager who is forced to adjust to a new and often unpleasant life after his parents are killed in a car crash. Major followed that novel with another that is even more hard-hitting: *Far from Shore*. That story, about a defiant but likable fifteen-year-old who has problems with alcohol and the police before accepting responsibility for his own life, won the Canadian Young Adult Book Award in 1981. Kevin Major's new novel, *Thirty-six Exposures*, reflects the setting and cultural backgrounds as well as the local dialect of the island of Newfoundland, a place previously unfamiliar to most American teen-agers.

Mr. Major lives with his wife and young son in Sandy Cove on Bonavista Bay, Newfoundland.

Kids from single-parent homes may sometimes have more difficulties than other kids. It's no easy job for single parents, either. Sometimes there is a clash between a parent and a teen-ager. In the following story Mrs. Brooks reveals how she feels about a serious problem she had with her daughter. . . .

AN ORDINARY WOMAN

BETTE GREENE

I dial the number that for more than twenty years has been committed to memory and then begin counting the rings. One . . . two . . . three . . . four . . . five . . . six—Christ! What's wrong with—

"Newton North High School, good morning."

"Jeannette? Oh, good morning. This is Armanda Brooks. Look, I may be a few minutes late today. Something came up—no, dear, I'm fine, thanks for asking. It's just a . . . a family matter that I must take care of. I shouldn't be more than ten to twenty minutes late for my first class, and I was wondering if you'd kindly ask one of my students, Dani Nikas, to start reading to the class from where we left off in *The Chocolate War?* . . . Oh, that would help a lot. . . . Thanks, Jeannette, thanks a lot."

Aimlessly I wander from bookcase to armchair to table and finally to the large French window that looks out upon my street. Like yesterday and so many yesterdays before, my neighbor's paneled station wagon is parked in the exact spot halfway up their blue asphalt driveway. And today, like yesterday, Roderick Street continues to be shaded by a combination of mature oaks and young Japanese maples.

How can everything look the same when nothing really

feels the same? Good Lord, Mandy Brooks, how old are you going to have to be before you finally get it into your head that the world takes no interest in your losses?

The grandfather clock in the hall begins chiming out the hour of seven and suddenly fear gnaws at my stomach. What am I afraid of now? For one thing, all those minutes. At least thirty of them that I'll have to face alone, here, with just my thoughts.

Calm down now! It's only thirty minutes. Why, the last thing the locksmith said last night was that he'd be here first thing this morning. "Between seven thirty and eight for sure!"

Anyway, nobody can make me think when I still have the kitchen counter to wipe and breakfast dishes to put into the dishwasher. Thinking hasn't come this hard since Steve's death on the eve of our eighteenth anniversary. That was major league pain all right, but so dear God is this. So is this. . . .

No time for that now—no time! Tidying up the kitchen is the only thing that I want to think about. But upon entering the kitchen, I see that with the exception of a mug still half full of undrunk coffee, there is really nothing to do. I pour the now cold coffee into the sink before examining the mug with all those miniature red hearts revolving around the single word MOM.

It was a gift from Caren and not all that long ago either. Maybe a year, but certainly no more than a year ago. But even then I had had suspicions that something wasn't right. Maybe without Caren's loving gift coming at me out of the blue, I would have followed my instincts and checked things out. But frankly I doubt that. The thing is that I wanted—needed—to believe in my daughter.

And going through her drawers in search of I-knew-not-what offended me. It goes against my sense that everybody, even a seventeen-year-old, deserves privacy.

You make me sick, Mandy Brooks, you really do! Just when did you get to be such a defender of the constitutional rights of minors? Why don't you at least have the courage to come on out and tell the truth. Say that, at all costs, you had to protect yourself from the truth. The terrible truth that your daughter, your lovely daughter is a junkie!

Stopit! Stopit! I'm not listening to you anymore! And there's nothing you can do to make me! Steve . . . Steve, oh my God, Steve, how I need you! There hasn't been a day, or even an hour, in all these twenty-two months since you left Caren and me that I haven't needed you. Don't believe those people who observe me from safe distances before patting my wrists and commenting on how strong I am. "How wonderfully you're carrying on alone."

Maybe I walk pretty much the same and talk pretty much the same, but, Steve, I don't feel the same. The moment I saw them close the coffin over you, Steve, I knew then what I know now. That the part of me that was most alive and loving got buried down there with you.

So you see, Steve, you've just got to find some way to help us because despite what people say, I'm not strong and I honestly don't know what to do. I look, but I can't find answers, only questions. More and more questions demanding answers: Where did I go wrong with our daughter? Was I too strict? Or too lenient? Did I love her too little . . . or did I love her too much?

Outside a truck door slams. I look at my watch. Five minutes after seven. Could he be here already? I rush to the window to see a white panel truck with black lettering —NEWTON CENTRE LOCKSMITHS—at my curb. And a young man, not all that much older than my seniors, is walking briskly up the front walk.

As he takes the front steps, two at a time, I already have the door open. "I really appreciate your being so prompt. You're even earlier than you said you'd be."

"It wasn't me you spoke to. It was my dad, but when he said that a Mrs. Brooks had to have her locks changed first thing in the morning so she wouldn't be late for school, well, I just knew it had to be you."

"Good Lord, I remember you!" I say, grabbing his hand. "You were a student of mine!"

He nods and smiles as he holds tightly to my hand. "You were my favorite English teacher." Then his eyes drop as though he is taking in the intricate pattern of the hall rug. "I guess you were my all-time favorite teacher!"

"Oh, that's lovely of you to say, David—your name is David?"

He grins as though I have given him a present. "David, yes. David Robinson. Hey, you know that's something! You must have had a few hundred students since me. I graduated Newton North two years ago. . . . How do you remember all of your students?"

I hear myself laughing. Laughter, it feels strange, but nice. Very nice. "You give me too much credit, you really do. I'm afraid I can't remember all my students. There have been so many in twenty years. But I think I can probably remember all the students that I really liked."

He takes in the compliment silently as I ask, "Your dad said it wouldn't take long putting in a new cylinder?"

"Ten minutes, Mrs. Brooks. Fifteen at the outside. . . . How many sets of keys will you need?"

"Sets of keys?" I feel my composure begin to dissolve. Suddenly I'm not sure I can trust my voice, so like an early grade-school child, I hold out a finger. Only one finger.

As I quickly turn to start up the stairs, the acrid smell of yesterday's fire once again strikes my nostrils. Never mind that now! This isn't the time for thinking about what was . . . and especially not the time for thinking about what could have been.

But even as I command myself to go nonstop into my bedroom for purse and checkbook and then quickly back down the stairs again, I see myself disobeying.

So I stand there at the threshold of Caren's room staring at the two things that had been burned by fire. Her canopy bed rests on only three legs and where the fourth leg once was there is a basketball-size burn in the thick lime-colored rug. Her stereo, records, wall-to-wall posters of rock stars, like everything else in this room, are layered with soot.

I remember now that one of the firemen remarked last night that it was sure a lucky thing that the fire had been contained before it reached the mattress. "You just don't know," he said, "how lucky you are."

How lucky I am? Am I lucky? That's what they used to call me back when I was a high school cheerleader. It all started when Big Joe Famori looked up from the huddle and didn't see me on the sidelines so he bellowed out, "Where's lucky Mandy?"

But if I really was lucky twenty-five years ago for Big Joe and the Malden Eagles, then why can't I be just a little lucky for the ones I've really loved? 'Cause with a little luck, Steve's tumor could just as easily have been benign, but it wasn't. And with a little luck, Caren could have got her highs from life instead of from drugs. But she didn't.

Luck. Dumb, unpredictable luck. Maybe there's no such thing as luck. Or maybe I used up all my precious supply on Big Joe Famori and the Malden Eagles. Is that where I failed you, Caren? Not having any more luck to give you?

When you were a little thing, I knew exactly how to make your tears go away. A fresh diaper, a bottle of warm milk, or maybe a song or two while you slept in my arms. That was all the magic I owned, but in your eyes, all power rested in my hands. For you, my love, I lit the stars at night and every morning called forth the eastern sun.

Probably very early on, I should have warned you that your mother was a very ordinary woman with not a single extraordinary power to her name. But, honey, I don't think you would have believed me because I think you needed me to be a miracle mom every bit as much as I needed to be one.

The trouble, though, didn't start until you grew larger and your needs, too, grew in size. And the all-protecting arms that I once held out to you couldn't even begin to cover these new and larger dimensions. Because it wasn't wet diapers or empty stomachs that needed attending to. It was, instead, pride that was shaken and dreams that somehow got mislaid.

So I see now that what from the very beginning I was dedicated to doing, became, of course, impossible to do. And maybe, just maybe, somewhere in the most submerged recesses of our brains, way down there where light or reason rarely penetrates, neither of us could forgive my impotence.

"Mrs. Brooks," David calls from downstairs. "You're all set now."

"I'll be right down." And then without moving from the spot at the threshold, I speak softly to the empty room. Or, more to the point, to the girl who once lived and laughed and dreamed within these walls. "Caren, dear Caren, I don't know if you're in the next block or the next state. I don't know if I'll see you by nightfall or if I'll see you ever.

"But if you someday return to slip your key into a lock that it no longer fits, I hope you'll understand. Understand, at least, that I'm not barring you, but only what you have become.

"You should know too that if I actually possessed just a little of that magic that you once believed in, I wouldn't have a moment's trouble deciding how to spend it. I'd hold you to me until your crying stops and your need for drugs fades away."

David Robinson stands at the bottom of the hall stairs, waiting for me. "You know, you're a lucky lady, Mrs. Brooks," he says, dropping a single brass key into my hand. "You're not even going to be late for class."

Although the center hall has always been the darkest room in the house, I fumble through my purse for my sunglasses before answering. "Yes, David," I say, peering at him through smoke-gray glasses. "People have always said that about me."

BETTE GREENE

Bette Greene is noted for the intense emotional connection that readers have with her novels. Although she grew up in a small Arkansas town, she studied in Paris and at Columbia University and now lives with her husband, twenty-year-old daughter, and sixteen-year-old son in Brookline, Massachusetts.

Her first novel, *Summer of My German Soldier,* which takes place during World War II in the heart of this country's Bible Belt, tells the true story of a Jewish girl who aides an escaped German prisoner of war. It's the story of their relationship and what happens when the world finds out. It was named an Outstanding Book of the Year by *The New York Times* in 1973 and was a National Book Award finalist. It also became an Emmy-winning made-for-television movie starring Kristy McNichol in the role of Patty Bergen. Later, Bette Greene wrote again about an older Patty Bergen in the award-winning *Morning Is a Long Time Coming.*

In 1975 Bette Greene won a Newbery Honor Book Award for *Philip Hall Likes Me. I Reckon Maybe,* which is a lighthearted account of a feisty young girl who likes Philip Hall *all* of the time while he likes her only some of the time. Beth's adventures with Philip Hall are further explored in *Get On Out of Here, Philip Hall!* and, most recently, in *I've Already Forgotten Your Name, Philip Hall!*

Published in 1983, *Them That Glitter and Them That Don't* is the story of Carol Ann Delaney, daughter of a gypsy fortune teller, who believes that she can use her singing and composing talents to become a country and western music star.

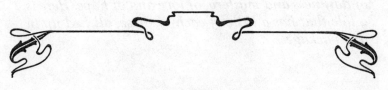

FAMILIES

*Every culture has its tales of bravery and adventure,
of darkness and mystery, of love and of hope. Here is
a tale that has a little of each of those, all tied up in
one package. . . .*

THE GIFT-GIVING

JOAN AIKEN

The weeks leading up to Christmas were always full of
excitement, and tremendous anxiety too, as the family
waited in suspense for the Uncles, who had set off in the
spring of the year, to return from their summer's travel-
ing and trading: Uncle Emer, Uncle Acraud, Uncle Gonfil,
and Uncle Mark. They always started off together, down
the steep mountainside, but then, at the bottom, they
took different routes along the deep narrow valley, Uncle
Mark and Uncle Acraud riding eastward, toward the great
plains, while Uncle Emer and Uncle Gonfil turned west,
toward the towns and rivers and the western sea.

Then, before they were clear of the mountains, they
would separate once more, Uncle Acraud turning south,
Uncle Emer taking his course northward, so that, the children occasionally thought, their family was scattered over
the whole world, netted out like a spider's web.

Spring and summer would go by in the usual occupations, digging and sowing the steep hillside garden beds,
fishing, hunting for hares, picking wild strawberries, making hay. Then, toward St. Drimma's Day, when the winds
began to blow and the snow crept down, lower and lower,
from the high peaks, Grandmother would begin to grow
restless.

Silent and calm all summer long she sat in her rocking
chair on the wide wooden porch, wrapped in a patchwork

comforter, with her blind eyes turned eastward toward the lands where Mark, her dearest and firstborn, had gone. But when the winds of Michaelmas began to blow, and the wolves grew bolder, and the children dragged in sacks of logs day after day, and the cattle were brought down to the stable under the house, then Grandmother grew agitated indeed.

When Sammle, the eldest granddaughter, brought her hot milk, she would grip the girl's slender brown wrist and demand: "Tell me, child, how many days now to St. Froida's Day?" (which was the first of December).

"Eighteen, Grandmother," Sammle would answer, stooping to kiss the wrinkled cheek.

"So many, still? So many till we may hope to see them?"

"Don't worry, Granny, the Uncles are *certain* to return safely. Perhaps they will be early this year. Perhaps we may see them before the feast of St. Melin" (which was December the fourteenth).

And then, sure enough, sometime during the middle weeks of December, their great carts would come jingling and trampling along the winding valleys. Young Mark (son of Uncle Emer), from his watchpoint up a tall pine over a high cliff, would catch the flash of a baggage-mule's brass brow-medal, or the sun glancing on the barrel of a carbine, and would come joyfully dashing back to report.

"Granny! Granny! The Uncles are almost here!"

Then the whole household, the whole village, would be filled with as much turmoil as that of a kingdom of ants when the spade breaks open their hummock. Wives would build the fires higher, and fetch out the best linen, wine, dried meat, pickled eggs; set dough to rising, mix cakes of honey and oats, bring up stone jars of preserved strawberries from the cellars; and the children, with the servants and half the village, would go racing down the perilous zigzag track to meet the cavalcade at the bottom.

The track was far too steep for the heavy carts, which would be dismissed and the carters paid off to go about their business. Then with laughter and shouting, amid a million questions from the children, the loads would be divided and carried up the mountainside on muleback, or on human shoulders. Sometimes the Uncles came home at night, through falling snow, by the smoky light of torches; but the children and the household always knew of their arrival beforehand, and were always there to meet them.

"Did you bring Granny's Chinese shawl, Uncle Mark? Uncle Emer, have you the enameled box for her snuff that Aunt Grippa begged you to get? Uncle Acraud, did you find the glass candlesticks? Uncle Gonfil, did you bring the books?"

"Yes, yes, keep calm, don't deafen us! Poor tired travelers that we are, leave us in peace to climb this devilish hill! Everything is there, set your minds at rest—the shawl, the box, the books—besides a few other odds and ends, pins and needles and fruit and a bottle or two of wine, and a few trifles for the village. Now, just give us a few minutes to get our breath, will you, kindly—" as the children danced round them, helping each other with the smaller bundles, never ceasing to pour out questions: "Did you see the Grand Cham? The Akond of Swat? The Fon of Bikom? The Seljuk of Rum? Did you go to Cathay? To Muskovy? To Dalai? Did you travel by ship, by camel, by llama, by elephant?"

And, at the top of the hill, Grandmother would be waiting for them, out on her roofed porch, no matter how wild the weather or how late the time, seated in majesty with her furs and patchwork quilt around her, while the Aunts ran to and fro with hot stones to place under her feet. And the Uncles always embraced her first, very fondly and respectfully, before turning to hug their wives and sisters-in-law.

Then the goods they had brought would be distributed through the village—the scissors, tools, medicines, plants, bales of cloth, ingots of metal, cordials, firearms, and musical instruments; after that there would be a great feast.

Not until Christmas morning did Grandmother and the children receive the special gifts that had been brought for them by the Uncles; and this giving always took the same ceremonial form.

Uncle Mark stood behind Grandmother's chair, playing on a small pipe that he had acquired somewhere during his travels; it was made from hard black polished wood, with silver stops, and it had a mouthpiece made of amber. Uncle Mark invariably played the same tune on it at these times, very softly. It was a tune that he had heard for the first time, he said, when he was much younger, once when he had narrowly escaped falling into a crevasse on the hillside, and a voice had spoken to him, as it seemed, out of the mountain itself, bidding him watch where he set his feet and have a care, for the family depended on him. It was a gentle, thoughtful tune, which reminded Sandri, the middle granddaughter, of springtime sounds, warm wind, water from melted snow dripping off the gabled roofs, birds trying out their mating calls.

While Uncle Mark played on his pipe, Uncle Emer would hand each gift to Grandmother. And she—here was the strange thing—she, who was stone-blind all the year long, could not see her own hand in front of her face, she would take the object in her fingers and instantly identify it. "A mother-of-pearl comb, with silver studs, for Tassy . . . it comes from Babylon. A silk shawl, blue and rose, from Hind, for Argilla. A wooden game, with ivory pegs, for young Emer, from Damascus. A gold brooch, from Hangku, for Grippa. A book of rhymes, from Paris, for Sammle, bound in a scarlet leather cover."

By stroking each gift with her old, blotched, clawlike fingers, frail as quills, Grandmother, who lived all the year round in darkness, could discover not only what the thing was and where it came from, but also the color of it, and that in the most precise and particular manner, correct to a shade. "It is a jacket of stitched and pleated cotton, printed over with leaves and flowers; it comes from the island of Haranati, in the eastern ocean; the colors are leaf-brown and gold and a dark, dark blue, darker than mountain gentians—" for Grandmother had not always been blind; when she was a young girl she had been able to see as well as anybody else.

"And this is for you, Mother, from your son Mark," Uncle Emer would say, handing her a tissue-wrapped bundle, and she would exclaim, "Ah, how beautiful! A coat of tribute silk, of the very palest green, so that the color shows only in the folds, like shadows on snow; the buttons and the button-toggles are of worked silk, lavender-gray, like pearl, and the stiff collar is embroidered with white roses."

"Put it on, Mother!" her sons and daughters-in-law would urge her, and the children, dancing 'round her chair, clutching their own treasures, would chorus, "Yes, put it on, put it on! Ah, you look like a queen, Granny, in that beautiful coat! The highest queen in the world! The queen of the mountain!"

Those months after Christmas were Grandmother's happiest time. Secure, thankful, with her sons safe at home, she would sit in the warm fireside corner of the big wooden family room. The wind might shriek, the snow gather higher and higher out of doors, but that did not concern her, for her family, and all the village, were well supplied with flour, oil, firewood, meat, herbs, and roots. The children had their books and toys, they learned lessons with the old priest, or made looms and spinning wheels, carved stools and chairs and chests with the tools their uncles had brought them. The Uncles rested and told tales of their travels; Uncle Mark played his pipe for hours together, Uncle Acraud drew pictures in charcoal of the places he had seen, and Granny, laying her hand on the paper covered with lines, would expound while Uncle Mark played: "A huge range of mountains, like wrinkled brown lines across the horizon; a wide plain of sand, silvery blond in color, with patches of pale, pale blue; I think it is not water but air the color of water. Here are strange lines across the sand where men once plowed it, long, long ago; and a great patch of crystal green, with what seems like a road crossing it. Now here is a smaller region of plum-pink, bordered by an area of rusty red. I think these are the colors of the earth in these territories; it is very high up, dry from height, and the soil glittering with little particles of metal."

"You have described it better than I could myself!" Uncle Acraud would exclaim, while the children, breathless with wonder and curiosity, sat cross-legged 'round her chair. And she would answer, "Yes, but I cannot see it at all, Acraud, unless your eyes have seen it first, and I cannot see it without Mark's music to help me."

"How does Grandmother *do* it?" the children would demand of their mothers, and Argilla, or Grippa, or Tassy would answer, "Nobody knows. It is Grandmother's gift. She alone can do it."

The people of the village might come in, whenever they chose, and on many evenings thirty or forty would be there, silently listening, and when Grandmother retired to bed, which she did early for the seeing made her weary, the audience would turn to one another with deep sighs, and murmur, "The world is indeed a wide place."

But with the first signs of spring the Uncles would become restless again, and begin looking over their equipment, discussing maps and routes, mending saddlebags and boots, gazing up at the high peaks for signs that the snow was in retreat.

Then Granny would grow very silent. She never asked them to stay longer, she never disputed their going, but her face seemed to shrivel, she grew smaller, wizened and huddled inside her quilted patchwork.

And on St. Petrag's Day, when the Uncles set off, when the farewells were said and they clattered off down the mountain through the melting snow and the trees with pink luminous buds, Grandmother would fall into a silence that lasted, sometimes, for as much as five or six weeks; all day she would sit with her face turned to the east, wordless, motionless, and would drink her milk and go to her bed-place at night still silent and dejected; it took the warm sun and sweet wild hyacinths of May to raise her spirits.

Then, by degrees, she would grow animated, and begin to say, "Only six months, now, till they come back."

But young Mark observed to his cousin Sammle, "It takes longer, every year, for Grandmother to grow accustomed."

And Sammle said, shivering though it was warm May weather, "Perhaps one year, when they come back, she will not be here. She is becoming so tiny and thin; you can see right through her hands, as if they were leaves." And Sammle held up her own thin brown young hand against the sunlight to see the blood glow under the translucent skin.

"I don't know how they would bear it," said Mark thoughtfully, "if when they came back we had to tell them that she had died."

But that was not what happened.

One December the Uncles arrived much later than usual. They did not climb the mountain until St. Misham's Day, and when they reached the house it was in silence. There was none of the usual joyful commotion.

Grandmother knew instantly that there was something wrong. "Where is my son Mark?" she demanded. "Why do I not hear him among you?" And Uncle Acraud had to tell her: "Mother, he is dead. Your son Mark will not come home, ever again."

"How do you *know?* How can you be *sure?* You were not there when he died?"

"I waited and waited at our meeting place, and a messenger came to tell me. His caravan had been attacked by wild tribesmen, riding north from the Lark Mountains. Mark was killed, and all his people. Only this one man escaped and came to bring me the story."

"But how can you be *sure?* How do you know he told the *truth?*"

"He brought Mark's ring."

Emer put it into her hand. As she turned it about in her thin fingers, a long moan went through her.

"Yes, he is dead. My son Mark is dead."

"The man gave me this little box," Acraud said, "which Mark was bringing for you."

Emer put it into her hand, opening the box for her. Inside lay an ivory fan. On it, when it was spread out, you could see a bird, with eyes made of sapphires, flying across a valley, but Grandmother held it listlessly, as if her hands were numb.

"What is it?" she said. "I do not know what it is. Help me to bed, Argilla. I do not know what it is. I do not wish to know. My son Mark is dead."

Her grief infected the whole village. It was as if the keystone of an arch had been knocked out; there was nothing to hold the people together.

That year spring came early, and the three remaining Uncles, melancholy and restless, were glad to leave on their travels. Grandmother hardly noticed their going.

Sammle said to Mark: "You are clever with your hands. Could you not make a pipe—like the one my father had?"

"*I?*" he said. "Make a pipe? Like Uncle Mark's pipe? Why? What would be the point of doing so?"

"Perhaps you might learn to play on it. As he did."

"*I?* Play on a pipe?"

"I think you could," she said. "I have heard you whistle tunes of your own."

"But where would I find the right kind of wood?"

"There is a chest, in which Uncle Gonfil once brought books and music from Leiden. I think it is the same kind of wood. I think you could make a pipe from it."

"But how can I remember the shape?"

"I will make a drawing," Sammle said, and she drew with a stick of charcoal on the whitewashed wall of the cowshed. As soon as Mark looked at her drawing he began to contradict.

"No! I remember now. It was not like that. The stops came here—and the mouthpiece was like this."

Now the other children flocked 'round to help and advise.

"The stops were farther apart," said Creusie. "And there were more of them and they were bigger."

"The pipe was longer than that," said Sandri. "I have held it. It was as long as my arm."

"How will you ever make the stops?" said young Emer.

"You can have my silver bracelets that Father gave me," said Sammle.

"I'll ask Finn the smith to help me," said Mark.

Once Mark had got the notion of making a pipe into his head, he was eager to begin. But it took him several weeks of difficult carving; the black wood of the chest proved hard as iron. And when the pipe was made, and the stops fitted, it would not play; try as he would, not a note could he fetch out of it.

Mark was dogged, though, once he had set himself to a task; he took another piece of the black chest and began again. Only Sammle stayed to help him now; the other children had lost hope, or interest, and gone back to their summer occupations.

The second pipe was much better than the first. By September, Mark was able to play a few notes on it; by October he was playing simple tunes made up out of his head.

"But," he said, "if I am to play so that Grandmother can see with her fingers—if I am to do *that*—I must remember your father's special tune. Can *you* remember it, Sammle?"

She thought and thought. "Sometimes," she said, "it seems as if it is just beyond the edge of my hearing—as if somebody were playing it, far, far away, in the woods. Oh, if only I could stretch my hearing a little farther!"

"Oh, Sammle! Try!"

For days and days she sat silent or wandered in the woods, frowning, knotting her forehead, willing her ears to hear the tune again; and the women of the household said, "That girl is not doing her fair share of the task."

They scolded her and set her to spin, weave, milk the goats, throw grain to the hens. But all the while she continued silent, listening, listening, to a sound she could not hear. At night, in her dreams, she sometimes thought she could hear the tune, and she would wake with tears on her cheeks, wordlessly calling her father to come back and play his music to her, so that she could remember it.

In September the autumn winds blew cold and fierce; by October snow was piled around the walls and up to the windowsills. On St. Felin's Day the three Uncles returned, but sadly and silently, without the former festivities; although, as usual, they brought many bales and boxes of gifts and merchandise. The children went down, as usual, to help carry the bundles up the mountain. The joy had gone out of this tradition, though, and they toiled silently up the track with their loads.

It was a wild, windy evening; the sun set in fire, the wind moaned among the fir trees, and gusts of sleet every now and then dashed in their faces.

"Take care, children!" called Uncle Emer as they skirted along the side of a deep gully, and his words were caught by an echo and flung back and forth between the rocky walls: "Take care—care—care—care—care . . ."

"Oh!" cried Sammle, stopping precipitately and clutching the bag that she was carrying. "I have it! I can remember it! *Now* I know how it went!"

And, as they stumbled on up the snowy hillside, she hummed the melody to her cousin Mark, who was just ahead of her.

"Yes, that is it, yes!" he said. "Or, no, wait a minute, that is not *quite* right—but it is close, it is very nearly the way it went. Only the notes were a little faster, and there were more of them—they went up, not down—before the ending tied them in a knot—"

"No, no, they went down at the end, I am almost sure—"

Arguing, interrupting each other, disputing, agreeing, they dropped their bundles in the family room and ran away to the cowhouse where Mark kept his pipe hidden.

For three days they discussed and argued and tried a hundred different versions; they were so occupied that they hardly took the trouble to eat. But at last, by Christmas morning, they had reached agreement.

"I *think* it is right," said Sammle. "And if it is not, I do not believe there is anything more that we can do about it."

"Perhaps it will not work in any case," said Mark sadly. He was tired out with arguing and practicing.

Sammle was equally tired, but she said, "Oh, it *must* work. Oh, let it work! Please let it work! For otherwise I don't think I can bear the sadness. Go now, Mark, quietly and quickly, go and stand behind Granny's chair."

The family had gathered, according to Christmas habit, around Grandmother's rocking chair, but the faces of the Uncles were glum and reluctant, their wives dejected and hopeless. Only the children showed eagerness, as the cloth-wrapped bundles were brought and laid at Grandmother's feet.

She herself looked wholly dispirited and cast down. When Uncle Emer handed her a slender, soft package, she received it apathetically, almost with dislike, as if she would prefer not to be bothered by this tiresome gift ceremony.

Then Mark, who had slipped through the crowd without being noticed, began to play on his pipe just behind Grandmother's chair.

The Uncles looked angry and scandalized; Aunt Tassy cried out in horror: "Oh, Mark, wicked boy, how *dare* you?" but Grandmother lifted her head, more alertly than she had done for months past, and began to listen.

Mark played on. His mouth was quivering so badly that it was hard to grip the amber mouthpiece, but he played with all the breath that was in him. Meanwhile, Sammle, kneeling by her grandmother, held, with her own warm young hands, the old, brittle ones against the fabric of the gift. And, as she did so, she began to feel what Grandmother felt.

Grandmother said softly and distinctly: "It is a muslin shawl, embroidered in gold thread, from Lebanon. It is colored a soft brick red, with pale roses of sunset pink, and thorns of silver-green. It is for Sammle . . ."

JOAN AIKEN

Author of more than fifty books for children and adults as well as for teen-agers, Joan Aiken was born in Rye, England, the daughter of famous American poet Conrad Aiken. Before devoting her full time to writing novels, stories, poems, and plays, Ms. Aiken worked for the British Broadcasting Corporation, then in the London office of the United Nations as a librarian. After marrying and raising two children, she became a features editor for *Argosy* magazine, then a copywriter for a large London advertising agency. She now lives alternately in New York City and her home in Sussex, England.

She is probably best known among American children as the author of the "Dido Twite" novels, among them *Nightbirds on Nantucket* and *The Wolves of Willoughby Chase* for which she won the Guardian Award for children's literature in 1969. She also received the Mystery Writers of America Edgar Allan Poe Award for *Night Fall*. Among her many stories of fantasy and horror are *Not What You Expected, A Bundle of Nerves, Go Saddle the Sea,* and *The Shadow Guests.*

Her most recent novels for adults are *The Girl from Paris* and *Foul Matter,* and for younger readers *The Stolen Lake* and *Bridle the Wind.* In addition, Joan Aiken has completed several collections of short stories. Among them are *A Touch of Chill: Tales for Sleepless Nights* and *A Whisper in the Night.* Ms. Aiken is currently working on a new novel for adults.

Starting with ancient fairy tales, stepmothers have usually been presented quite negatively. Gogi's stepmother is no exception. But Gogi is determined to outwit her stepmother. . . .

SHE

ROSA GUY

"Just where do you think you're going?" she said.

"To the bathroom," I said.

"No, you're not," she said. "Not before you wash up these dishes."

"This is a matter of urgent necessity," I said. I hated that even my going to the bathroom had to be questioned.

"Don't want to hear," she said. "I'm sick and tired of emergency, emergency every night after dinner. Get to that sink."

"I'll wash the dishes," Linda said. She got up and started to clear off the table. I slipped out of the kitchen. The angry voice followed me down the hall:

"Linda, don't keep letting your sister get away with everything."

"I don't mind—really, Dorine," Linda said.

"That girl's just too damn lazy. . . ." I shut the bathroom door to muffle the sounds of her grievances against me. She didn't like me. She never had. And I didn't care. Stepmothers . . . !

Searching the bottom of the hamper for the science fiction magazine I had hidden beneath the dirty clothes, I sat on the toilet and began to read to get out of this world —as far from her as I could get.

From the day she had walked into our house she'd been on me. I was lying on my bed reading when she and

Daddy pushed into my room without knocking. Our eyes locked. She didn't speak. Neither did I.

I was in a panic. Daddy had forbidden me to read fairy tales. "At twelve years old! You too old," he'd said. He wanted me to read only school books. I hadn't had time to hide the book of fairy tales beneath my mattress as I usually did. I curled up around it, praying to keep his eyes from it.

But Daddy was only showing her the apartment. So she had to turn to inspect my almost bare room. When she looked back at me, her eyes said: What are you doing reading in this miserable room instead of doing something useful around this terrible house? My eyes answered: What's it to you?

They left the room the way they'd come. Abruptly. Hearing their footsteps going toward the kitchen, I got up and followed. Linda was in the kitchen, washing fish for our dinner. When they went in, Linda looked up and smiled.

"What a lovely girl," Dorine said, and the shock of her American accent went through me. What was Daddy doing with an American woman! "She's got to be the prettiest child I ever did see. My name is Dorine," she said.

From the first she had chosen Linda over me. Maybe because Linda was pretty, with her long, thick hair and clear brown eyes and brown velvet skin. I was plain-looking. Or maybe because Linda was two years older—already a teen-ager.

"You're Daddy's friend," Linda said, batting her long black eyelashes the way she always did whenever someone paid her a compliment. "I didn't know Daddy had a lady friend." Daddy gave Linda a quick look and she changed to: "My name is Linda. And that's"—she pointed to where I stood in the doorway—"the baby. Her name is Gogi."

But Dorine had already turned away from Linda to inspect the kitchen. And suddenly I saw our kitchen and the sweat of embarrassment almost drowned me: the sink was leaking and had a pan under it to catch the dirty water; the windowpanes were broken and stuffed with newspapers to keep out winter; the linoleum was worn, showing the soft wood beneath.

And she wore furs. Our mother had never worn furs. Not even when Daddy had had lots of money. People from the tropics didn't think of wearing things like furs. And the way Dorine looked around—nose squinched up, mouth pulled back—judging us, West Indians.

Daddy stood in the middle of the kitchen, quieter than usual—big, broad, handsome in his black overcoat, around his arm the black crepe band of mourning. His hands were deep in the pockets of his gray wool suit. And she hit out at him: "Damn, Harry, how can you live like this!"

Linda stopped smiling then. Daddy's eyebrows quivered. My mouth got tight with satisfaction. Daddy had a mean temper. I waited for him to blast her out of our house and out of our lives. She had socked us where we hurt—our pride.

"How you mean?" Daddy had said. "We ain't live so. You see mi restaurant. . . ." So, he had known her while our mother was still alive. ". . . I lose it," he said. "Mi wife dead. I sell mi house, mi furniture, mi car. I—I—mi friend let me stay here for a time—but it only for a short time." He was begging! I hated that he stood there begging.

"If it's only one minute, that's one minute too damn long," she said.

Lifting my head from the science fiction magazine to turn a page, I heard the sounds of pots banging against pans in the kitchen. And I heard Dorine's footsteps in the hall. I waited for the knob to turn on the bathroom door. She sometimes did that. But this time she went on into the living room. A short time later I heard the television playing.

It had been two years since the pointing, the ordering, the arranging and rearranging of our lives had begun. She had forced us to leave our old free apartment and move

into her big one with its big rooms, its big kitchen and all
those dozens of pots and pans for all things and all occasions. We had to listen to her constant: "Cleanliness is next
to godliness," and "A good housekeeper has a place for
everything and keeps everything in its place." Like who
told her that what we wanted most in life was to be house-
keepers? I didn't!

Daddy let her get away with everything. He stayed out
most days looking for work. And he spent evenings gam-
bling with his friends. The times he spent at home he
spent with her—laughing and joking in their bedroom.
She entertained him to keep him there. I'd see her flash-
ing around the house in her peach-colored satin dressing
gown, her feet pushed into peach-colored frilly mules, her
big white teeth showing all across her face, her gown
falling away to expose plump brown knees. Guess that's
what he liked—that combination of peach satin and
smooth brown skin.

She worked, a singer. Sometimes for weeks she'd be out
on the road. Then she'd come home with her friends and
they'd do all that loud American talking and laughing. She
sometimes brought us lovely things back from "the road."
Blouses, underwear, coats. She won Linda's affection like
that and might have won mine if I hadn't heard a man
friend say to her one day: "Dorine, it's bad enough you got
yourself hooked up with that West Indian. But how did
you manage to get in a family way?"

"Big Red," she called him. "I'm in love."

"With all of 'em?" he asked.

"They come with the deal," she said.

"Some deal," he answered.

"You don't need to worry none, Big Red," she said.
"They earns their keep."

She saw me standing in the doorway then, and her big
eyes stretched out almost to where I stood. Guilty. Her
mouth opened. I walked away. I had heard enough. I
went right in and told Linda. "That's what she wants us
around for," I said. "To be her maids."

"Gogi," Linda said. "She probably didn't mean it that way at all."

"What other way could she mean it?" I asked. Innocent Linda. She never saw the evil in the hearts and minds of people.

But from that day Dorine picked on me. When I vacuumed the hall, she called me to show me specks I could hardly see and made me vacuum over again. When I cleaned my room, she went in and ran her fingers over the woodwork to show me how much dust I had left behind. "That ain't the way we do things around here," she liked to say. "Do it right or don't do it at all." As though I had a choice!

"Trying to work me to death, that's what she's doing," I complained to Linda.

"But why don't you do things right the first time, Gogi?" Linda said. I could only stare at her. My sister!

We had always been close. Linda hadn't minded doing things for me before Dorine came, as long as I read to her. Linda never had time for things like reading. She knew she was pretty and kept trying to make herself perfect. Linda washed her blouses and underwear by hand. She ironed her clothes to defeat even the thought of a wrinkle. And she had always done mine along with hers, just to have me read to her.

But now our stepmother who had turned our father against us had turned my sister against me! Well, if Linda wanted to be a maid, that was her business. I did enough when I vacuumed the hall and cleaned my room. If Linda had to take Dorine's side against me, then let Dorine read for her. I was satisfied to do my reading to myself—by myself.

Sitting too long on the toilet, I felt the seat cut into my thighs. I got up to unstick myself and leaving the toilet unflushed—not to give away that I had finished—I sat on the closed stool, listening to what ought to have been sounds of glass clinking against glass, of china against china.

The quiet outside the bathroom unsettled me. I usually knew when Linda had finished with the dishes. I always heard when she passed to join Dorine in the living room. They played the television loud, thinking to make me jealous, making me feel unneeded, pretending not to care that I had shut myself from them and that I might go to my room without even a goodnight. But I hadn't heard Linda pass!

The television kept playing. I strained to hear the program to tell the time. It was on too low. Getting up, I thought of going out to see how things were but sat down again. Better to give Linda a little more time. I started another story.

I had only half finished when my concentration snapped. The television had been turned off. I tried to but couldn't get back into the story. Instead I sat listening, hoping to pick up sounds from the silent house. What time was it?

Getting up, I put my ear to the door. No outside sound. Unlocking the door, I cracked it open and peeked out. The hallway was dark! Everybody had gone to bed! How late was it? Taking off my shoes I started tiptoeing down toward my room. Then from the dark behind me I heard: "Ain't no sense in all that creeping. Them dishes waiting ain't got no ears." I spun around. A light went on and there she was, lying on a chaise longue that had been pulled up to the living room door. "That's right, it's me," she said. "And it's one o'clock in the morning. Which gives you enough time to wash every dish in the sink squeaking clean before one o'clock noon."

Tears popped to my eyes as she marched me down past my room, past the room where Linda slept, into the kitchen. Tears kept washing my cheeks as I washed dishes. She sat inspecting every one, acting as though we were playing games. If we were, I expected it to go on forever. She had tricked me—and she had won.

ROSA GUY

Born in Trinidad, Rosa Guy grew up in Harlem, New York. Although she was an orphan and a high school drop-out, she went on to study at New York University and to help found the Harlem Writers Guild.

She is the author of a trilogy about three young black women, starting with *The Friends*, an American Library Association Notable Book. A West Indian family named Cathy plays a dominant role in that book as well as in *Ruby* and *Edith Jackson*, both selected as Best Books for Young Adults by the ALA.

Ms. Guy is also the author of a series of young adult novels about Imamu Jones, an intelligent, street-wise school drop-out who becomes a self-appointed detective. *The Disappearance*, an ALA Best Book for Young Adults, was the first novel about Imamu, who is falsely accused of murder. That was followed by *New Guys Around the Block*, in which Imamu and a brilliant friend attempt to solve a series of crimes that baffle the experts. Imamu is involved in another murder case in the third book in the series, *And I Heard a Bird Sing*.

In addition, Rosa Guy translated and adapted *Mother Crocodile* from "Maman Caïman" by Birago Diop, a story for children beautifully illustrated by John Steptoe, and wrote *Mirror of Her Own*, a story about power, class differences, and discrimination as it affects both blacks and whites.

Rosa Guy has lived in Rome, Haiti, and Senegal as well as in Trinidad, and now makes her home in New York City, where she continues to write about class differences in American society.

Certain sounds, special smells, distinctive objects, can bring back memories from our childhood. For one ordinary man, the summer heat usually brings memories of his father. But on this one day those memories are mixed with the pain of his wife's death and with concern for the feelings of his teen-age son. . . .

IN THE HEAT

ROBERT CORMIER

I always see my father in the heat waves, and I think back to my tenement childhood and how it was in the evenings when everybody sat on the piazzas or the back steps, the women fanning themselves with their moist after-supper aprons and the men arguing languidly about the Red Sox or the piecework rates at the comb shops while the kids, myself among them, found energy enough for Kick The Can or Rotten Eggs although it was too hot for Buck Buck, How Many Fingers Up? One night, my father went to Baker's and returned with six of those two-for-a-nickel ice-cream cones for my mother, my brothers, my sisters, and me, and a bottle of beer for himself: a magnificent gesture in the parchness of the Depression on a night that wasn't paynight. And still later—or perhaps it was another evening altogether—my father again performed an act of splendor. My mother had called us in, her voice halting our adventures, but my father stood up on the steps and yelled: "Hell, let them stay out, Ellie. Who wants to go to sleep in this heat?" I loved him at that moment with a love that took me by surprise and left me astonished, awed by the fact that he understood how a kid never wants to go to bed. In my memories, it seems that we never went to bed at all that night but remained outside in the hushed intimacy of the heat.

Now a heat wave assaults the city but I give my father only a fleeting thought. There are other things to think about, although I try to keep my mind from them. Not things, really. Only one: the fact of Ruth's death. I sit in the living room and try not to think of anything.

Richy comes down the stairs from his bedroom and stands at the doorway. He is on the point of strangling in his shirt and tie. "This all right?" he asks. He has found a somber tie. Usually, his taste runs to wild colors.

"I'd forget the jacket," I say. "Carry it on your arm. The . . . the place is air-conditioned. Put it on when you get there."

"Okay," he says. He stands there waiting.

He's tall for his age, fifteen, gaining weight finally after shooting up like an arrow in the past year. He is ordinarily a witty lighthearted kid. Recently, he discovered the English language and has run amok with puns. One night when I wanted to use the heating pad for relieving my aching shoulder and found that it wasn't working, he told me: "You can't have your ache and heat it too." I had winced as you must whenever someone concocts a pun, although I chuckled to myself. Across a bridge of puns, Richy and I were able to meet. But there have been no puns in the last few weeks. And at this moment, all we have in common, all that we can share, is a dead woman: my wife, his mother. In a few minutes, we will view her body at the funeral home. A custom I deplore but one that convention decrees. Richy has never visited a funeral home. We tried to protect him from that kind of thing. He has never seen his mother dead, either, something from which there is no protection.

The heat is terrible.

"You ready, Dad?" he asks.

"Give me a minute."

I have been ready all day. I have done nothing today but wait for it all to be over. My mother arrived early this morning. To help. She prepared a breakfast that Richy and I barely touched. She made the beds and dusted furniture. She took out the vacuum cleaner but I told her to put it away. The heat hammered at the house and the walls seemed to be buckling. The vacuum cleaner, for Christ's sake. My mother began to cry, huge tears filling her cheeks' crevices, her mouth askew, her eyes desperate. I wanted to comfort my mother who wanted to comfort me but the language was all wrong. Ironing boards, hearty breakfasts, vacuum cleaners—that's her language, that's how she communicates—but I have no language at all at the moment. I am mute, illiterate at communication. Later, my brothers and sisters either visited or called on the telephone and I listened and spoke words and then listened again but it didn't mean anything.

Now Richy waits for me and I go to the front hall and open the closet. My fingers flick lightly over her things. I ignore the disreputable jacket she wore when she puttered around outside on chilly days and the crazy plaid raincoat she bought on impulse and hated once she got it home. During the months of her illness, knowing its hopelessness, I have prepared myself for these encounters. What I dread are the reminders, waiting like unexploded time bombs in unexpected places. This morning, I discovered one of her bobby pins on the mantel. I stared at it awhile, remembering last winter's fires. Then I poured myself a drink. Scotch on the rocks at ten thirty in the morning. I can handle the clothes, the lipsticks in the bathroom and the jars on her vanity. But I shudder at the things I can't anticipate.

I select the proper suit jacket. I wonder idly if my breath carries souvenirs of all the whiskey I drank today and think: What the hell. The whiskey had been a waste. It hadn't done a thing: it had reached only my stomach.

Outside, the sun glints dazzlingly on the crimson automobile. I am embarrassed driving a red car to a funeral home. The car has been baking all day in the sun, and its hoarded heat assails us as we enter. The air is blistered.

The plastic seat covers penetrate my clothes. I touch the steering wheel and the metal stings. I leave my hands there for a moment, absorbing the pain. I offer it up for her: ridiculous. Perhaps the whiskey has done its job after all. I am suddenly giddy but the sound of the motor establishes balance again.

Richy is pale despite the heat and the tight collar.

"Take it easy," I say. "I've arranged everything as easily as possible."

He nods, looking straight ahead.

"Your mother didn't believe in this kind of thing and neither do I. But there are conventions. It'll only last an hour and a half. Seven to eight thirty."

"What do we do?"

"Nothing, really. People come and offer their sympathy. Friends and relatives. You and I—we stand there and shake their hands. And say: thank you. I don't know. Maybe there's some kind of therapy in it."

We drive slowly through the streets. The heat has driven people inside to their air-conditioners. In the old days, hot weather drew people outdoors in search of an errant breeze. One morning, my father and I climbed the steps to the roof of the three-story tenement building where we lived. He was wearing one of those undershirts you seldom see anymore, not a T-shirt but the kind that looks like the top of an old-fashioned bathing suit. Anyway, he and I stood there at dawn and the air was as fresh as an apple split in two. "Too bad we can't bottle this stuff," my father said, inhaling. Everyone in the house, in the neighborhood, in the world was asleep but my father and I sniffed morning breezes together. I had never been on the roof before: it was mysterious and wonderful.

"Dad," Richy says.

"Yes," I answer. Don't ask me anything hard.

"Did she suffer much?"

"No," I say. "Not physical pain." Hoping he doesn't catch the qualifier. Her death was expected, the illness terminal, the details of which I constantly push from the forefront of my mind. Because of modern medicine, her body was spared pain. She merely grew weaker and smaller, shriveling away on the high hospital bed. Toward the end, despite her brave countenance, her insistent smiles, I knew that she knew. One day she said: *I'm so humiliated.* Her complexion had been flawless and even the sun could not alter its loveliness but only deepened its glow. She loved the sun. Once, early in March, I arrived home from work to find her in a bathing suit, a sheet of aluminum against the house to reflect the sun. "You're a nut," I told her, "it's not spring yet."

The sun now is hemorrhaging to death in the back of the buildings they are tearing down on Mechanic Street for the urban renewal program. The structures resemble decayed teeth. I tell myself to think of something cheerful. We drive by the church but I don't look. I refuse to dwell on the day we were married there or the Sunday of Richy's christening. I haven't prayed for a long time. At first, I prayed a lot and then I didn't pray at all.

At the funeral home, my brother Ernie's station wagon is parked near the entrance. He has driven my other brother and two sisters as well as my mother to the place. There is no one here from Ruth's family. Her parents are dead and her only sister is an invalid living in Arizona, unable to travel. I am glad that she is being spared all this. I had hoped to spare my mother the ordeal because I know it reminds her of my father's death, even though he died almost five years ago, in deep winter, the funeral held in a howling blizzard. I had approached my mother tentatively about having the funeral immediately after Ruth's death. No calling hours. "My God," she said. "What will people think?" I had compromised: ninety minutes, no more.

Ernie meets me at the door, looking concerned. The undertaker had suggested that we arrive fifteen minutes early in order to have a few private moments together. We are five minutes late. The door swings open and chilled air sucks us into the foyer. It's as if I have been drenched with ice water, and my body is instantly damp, oozing perspiration. My shirt clings to my back.

The worst moment, of course, is when Richy and I advance to the casket. The array of flowers stuns the eye but their beauty is refrigerated, antiseptic. We confront the casket but I avert my eyes. I don't want to look at her: there is no point. We kneel for a moment and I am terrified for Richy. The last time he saw his mother, she was a wan wasted figure in the hospital. And now this artificial thing surrounded by scentless flowers.

As we rise from the kneeler, I touch Richy's shoulder and he blinks his eyes rapidly at me, as if tapping out some private Morse code. He nods his head: I have the impression that he is trying to reassure me. We have no time to speak because the people begin to arrive. Richy and I stand there, slightly to the right of the casket. Faces pass before us and hands thrust themselves at us and murmurs of sympathy whisper in our ears. At one point, Father Norton appears and we pray. The air-conditioner hums a continuous Amen. People stream in now. I am surprised at their number: from the office, old friends, nodding acquaintances, Ruth's friends. An old man with foul breath shakes my hand, grunting sympathy: someone Ruth had casually befriended perhaps. She was always striking up conversations with total strangers, particularly in supermarkets. Once, she received a black eye trying to break up a fight between two kids on the sidewalk. Thinking of that poor bruised cheek, I glance involuntarily toward the casket and see her at last. I look for a long time. A blizzard of hands interrupts me: Richy's classmates have arrived in a delegation and they swirl around us. But even when I turn away I still see her there in the casket. I wait for the reaction but there is none. I shiver in the sterile, chilled air. My grief has not diminished but I realize that a peak has been reached: it can go no higher. Perhaps the peak was reached this morning when I found her bobby pin and needed that whiskey.

At last, it is over. The people have left. My family gathers for a final prayer, and Richy and I kneel there once again. I submit myself to a scrutiny of the stranger lying before me, because Ruth is far removed from all this, and it does not matter. What matters is Richy: I feel him tense beside me. I am the first one to rise and the others follow. My eyes want to seek Richy's but the undertaker hovers nearby and my mother is weeping softly and insisting at the same time that Richy and I spend the remainder of the evening at her house where the family and some close friends will gather. She has been baking all afternoon. My brother Ernie wants to know what he can do to help. "Nothing," I say. I only want to get Richy out of here. I promise to meet them at my mother's house later and guide Richy to the door.

I had forgotten the heat but it assails us as we step outside, although dusk has blunted its sharpness. The car has cooled off a little. The discomfort now is from the contrast between the air conditioning and the outdoor air.

Richy and I have not spoken since leaving the others.

"How do you feel?" I ask as my foot nudges the accelerator into action.

"All right," he says.

"Let's ride awhile." I think how nice it would be to find a rooftop somewhere.

Richy murmurs something but I don't quite hear because of the traffic noises. I lean toward him. "What did you say?"

"I said: you didn't look at her for a long time. Not until toward the end."

My silence is confirmation.

"I know why," he says, after a while.

I wait for him to go on.

"Because—because that wasn't her back there," he says.

I wait for a traffic light to turn from red to green. A girl in a small foreign car in the next lane guns her motor, rehearsing her getaway when the light changes. Suddenly, she races ahead of us and the fellow behind me blows his horn.

"And in the bed at the end, that wasn't her either," I say.

I swerve away from Main Street and head for the outskirts where the pace is less hectic and the darkness is not interrupted by neon flashes, car headlights.

"Know how I think of her, Dad?"

I notice that my knuckles are no longer white where they grip the steering wheel. "How?" I ask.

"With all that crazy junk she used to put on to get a tan," he says.

"She was a nut about the sun," I say.

"But know what I remember most, Dad? One night at the Cape on vacation when you'd been invited out to a big dance or something by the man that owned the yacht. Mom came into the room, whirling around, and she was wearing something, I don't know, kind of off the shoulder . . ."

"Sexy," I offer, pondering the risk of sacrilege.

"Yeah," he says. And the sacrilege does not exist. "Ted Harding was at the cottage, remember? And Ted said: 'Hey, your mother's ice.' That was the big word that year: *ice.* Beyond *cool.* And then later that night you and Mom came in—it must've been about two o'clock—and you were both laughing soft and kind of giggling. You put a record on, and I sneaked out of my bedroom and watched. You were dancing. Her eyes were closed and she looked, I don't know, happy. . . ."

My father died in the winter, with winds howling outside, and he fought until the end, raging in his bed, battling the black thing that beat against the windows. But I have always remembered him in the summer's heat. On the piazza steps. On the roof. Handing out those ice-cream cones. Saying, "Hell, let them stay out, Ellie." A man much taller than his height.

I look at Richy and his face is in shadow. We pass a

streetlight and his features leap to life. My heart is Hiroshima and I expect it to be, but a son's memories should be
things of comfort.

I turn the car back toward the town. I want to drive by
the church. I want to see my mother and my brothers and
my sisters. I want to drive on the streets of my childhood
again and see once more that old tenement building
where I was a boy, in the summer, in the heat.

ROBERT CORMIER

The world of books for teen-agers was changed forever when Robert Cormier published *The Chocolate War* in 1974. Prior to that, Mr. Cormier had published three novels for adults. But it was *The Chocolate War* that gained attention because of its exceptional writing, painful conflict, and downbeat ending.

While *The Chocolate War* provides insights into school violence and the struggle of one boy to be an individual, Cormier's *I Am the Cheese* shows the frightening realities of a family having to change its identity because of a father's heroic act against corruption, an act that endangers the lives of the entire family. Corruption, betrayal, and personal heroism hit their highest peaks in *After the First Death* when a small group of terrorists hijacks a busload of children. His most recent novel—*The Bumblebee Flies Anyway*—concerns the grim but determined life of several teen-agers in a special hospital for the terminally ill. All of his thought-provoking novels for teen-agers have been named Best Books of the Year by the American Library Association, and *I Am the Cheese* was made into a movie starring Hope Lange, Robert Wagner, and Robert Macnaughton.

Like the father in "In the Heat," Robert Cormier is a gentle, thoughtful, family-oriented man. For many years he was a prizewinning newspaper writer and editor for the *Fitchburg Sentinel* in Massachusetts, writing upbeat stories and providing glimpses of life in a small town. He presents similar views of teen-agers and parents in his collected short stories, *8 Plus 1*. Cormier, who has raised three daughters and a son, lives with his wife in Leominster, Massachusetts, where he continues to work on the sequel to *The Chocolate War.*

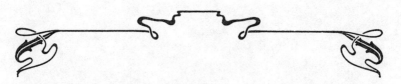

GOING INTO AND
BEYOND
THE STORIES

To Readers:

The questions that follow are intended to help you think about some of the key issues and concepts in the stories you have read. In some cases you may be able to appreciate the stories more by examining their form. Because different readers have different reactions and therefore different interpretations of what they have read, you might enjoy discussing some of your reactions with your friends or classmates.

Similarly, the suggestions for writing may provide you with opportunities to express yourself in other ways besides classroom or informal talk. Don't let the writing be a chore. Write in a relaxed but intentional way. Above all be honest and try to be creative.

Through these activities you can get deeper into and go beyond the stories you have enjoyed.

To Teachers:

If you wish to utilize these questions in your classrooms, please use them for purposes of exploration. These are not intended as questions for quizzes or essay tests. They have been designed for discussion and writing to explore meanings, examine forms, and evaluate ideas in these stories in particular and in short stories in general.

I, HUNGRY HANNAH CASSANDRA GLEN . . .

• What clues are there that this story takes place in recent times? In what ways is this story timeless?

• How strong is the friendship between Hannah and Crow? Will they eventually develop a romantic relationship?

• What do the children's wills reveal about each of them?

• If Hannah wasn't related to Mr. Francher, why did he act so friendly toward her? Why didn't Mrs. Francher act the same way?

• The kids have mixed feelings about going to the funeral and the wake. Why do they think that maybe they shouldn't go; why do they think they should? What is ironic about their stuffing themselves at the story's end?

• Norma Mazer utilizes several similes throughout her story to leave clear and interesting images in the minds of the reader—e.g. "his face looked as if it had been splashed with gobs of rusty paint." And the sisters looked "like two swollen black balloons." Write a description of someone you know, using similes to describe that person's looks and mannerisms.

MAY I HAVE YOUR AUTOGRAPH?

• Who seems to be the more typical teen-ager, Wendy or Rosalind? What evidence supports your opinion?

• Why is Wendy so sure of herself? Is that self-assurance typical of teen-agers?

• In most friendships, one person is often stronger, more assertive. Which one is more dominant in this pair? What contributions does the other make to their friendship?

• Why do you suppose Marjorie Sharmat did not let

Wendy tell her own story? What's the difference between Rosalind's perspective and the perspective Wendy might have given?

• Using popular magazines and other library resources, make a list of the habits and quirks of your favorite rock star or other media personality. Other than at a show or a public appearance, where might you likely find that person? Write a description of that individual's habits and typical behaviors.

• Write a story about an adventure you had with one of your friends. Try to choose something that reveals some aspect of your friendship with each other.

MIDNIGHT SNACK

• How have the unicorns been affected by having to live in the subways? What is so special about the shy ones? What is likely to happen to them in the future?

• What is the relationship between Beth and Jerry at the beginning of the story? How has it changed by the end of the story? What exactly has caused that change?

• Why does Jerry sniff and wipe his nose after the unicorn touches his hand? What does Beth see in Jerry that Jerry doesn't know she sees?

• Why doesn't Beth tell Jerry about her father's feelings about the unicorns?

• Beth says: "Nothing that lives in a subway should be that proud, and that hungry, and feel that helpless. Nothing that lives *anywhere* should." Is Diane Duane making a political statement there? How do you feel about authors making such statements in their stories?

• Unicorns have always been considered magical. Write an essay that might appear in your school or local newspaper that states your opinions about unicorns or about people who love the idea of unicorns.

PIGEON HUMOR

• Why was the chauffeur the only one dressed in black?

• Why does Tracy have mixed feelings about her father's death?

• What words describe Tracy's mother? How has her mother helped or hindered Tracy's adjustment to the death?

• We are told that Tracy "hadn't thought a funeral could be so noisy." In this case, what was the purpose of the "noise"? What is the result of the noise later at the school concert?

• Of what importance are teddy bears to Tracy? What do they represent to her?

• What is the significance of the tune the children try to sing? Why does that particular number affect Tracy the way it does?

• Is there hope for Tracy that the pain will someday stop? What might help to ease the pain for her?

• If she were asked to give advice to divorced parents about how they could help their children cope better, what might Tracy say? Write her advice to parents as if she is a teen-age Dear Abby.

PRISCILLA AND THE WIMPS

• Why do people like Monk think they are so special? What allows people like them to be so powerful?

• Although the narrator's purpose is to tell about Monk and Priscilla, he reveals a lot about himself in the process. What do you know about his personality, attitudes, and social standing?

• How do the names fit the personalities of each character in the story?

• What do you think eventually happened to Monk?

• Write an article for your school newspaper, giving students advice on how to avoid conflicts with guys like Monk Klutter.

• As if you are Priscilla, describe your feelings about being so big. Explain also why you usually don't say much.

WELCOME

• In what part of the country does this story take place? What details lead you to that conclusion?

• Why are Tina, her mother, and Aunt Dessie going to Noella's house?

• Although we never meet Sharon, she plays an important role in this story. What is Ouida Sebestyen's purpose in introducing her? How are Sharon's problems like those of Mary and Tina?

• When she first meets Tina, Noella hugs her and Tina says: "Then I was inside that root-hold, as helpless as a rock being broken by long gentle pressure." How does that foreshadow what happens later in the story?

• What is the significance of what happens between Tina and Arley?

• Tina accuses her mother of "collecting little keys that lock out the things in your life that scare you." What does Tina try to lock out of her own life? What does she eventually realize?

• Sebestyen uses a lot of colorful descriptions: e.g. "tears as hard as hailstones"; "a square unpainted house smothering under a trumpet vine"; "a little dried-apple woman." Write a description of a place you've visited—perhaps the home of a relative you don't visit very often. Use colorful descriptions to describe the place and the person you visited.

FUTURE TENSE

- How many different meanings can you find in the title?
- Did Gary's observations convince you that his English teacher was an alien? What specific evidence did he use to persuade himself that Mr. Smith was an alien?
- Why did Gary keep revising his composition? Is that typical of most high school writers?
- What implications about writing is Robert Lipsyte giving to students through this story?
- Some people enjoy reading science fiction a lot; others hate it. What makes you like it or not like it?
- What will become of Gary? Write the next scene in which Gary arrives on the alien planet. How is he received? How does he react?
- Like Gary did, write your description of a typical day at school, in which you strut *your* sentences, parade *your* paragraphs.

TURMOIL
IN A BLUE AND BEIGE BEDROOM

- Of what significance is the color of the room?
- Although there is no description of the physical or personality characteristics of the speaker in the story, we know what she looks like, how she acts, and what things are important to her. How does Judie Angell accomplish that?
- Some people might accuse this girl of being *fickle*. What does she do that would lead them to that conclusion?

• If you were John, knowing what you now know about this girl, would you ask her out again? What would contribute to your decision?

• Why does this character not have a name we know?

• What does the author do to make the girl's statements sound so realistic?

• How do you know what the person on the other end of the phone has said?

• Make a recording of your side of a phone conversation with a friend, then listen to see what aspects of your personality and your attitudes are revealed.

FURLOUGH—1944

• Are Jack and Dottie really in love? How can you tell?

• What does Dottie admire and want from a man? What does Jack admire and want from a woman?

• Both Jack and Dottie are very shy people. Is it likely that some young men and women today are that shy, or were kids in the '40s more likely to be that way? Do older teen-agers today have relationships like the one in this story, or are they likely to behave differently?

• In what ways is the setting important in this story? What objects, expressions, and events in the story are characteristics of the 1940s?

• After Jack gets to England, but before he goes into battle, he writes several letters. Write a letter that Jack might have written to Dottie expressing his feelings about the day they spent together.

• Write the dialogue that Greenie and Selma might have after they leave Jack and Dottie at the beach, showing what each thinks of the two young lovers.

DO YOU WANT MY OPINION?

• At what point in the story did you realize that it takes place in a future time?

• This is one of the shortest stories in this collection, yet it has a lot to say. What impressions do you have about John's father? What kind of relationship does John have with his father? What subjects seem to be most important in John's school? Why is John so attracted to Lauren? What values are important in John's society?

• In what ways does life in John's school differ from life in your school? How is it alike?

• Why does John think he's abnormal? Is he? Is it common for today's teen-agers to feel the same way? What seems to cause that?

• Explain how the graffiti on the bathroom walls illustrates the theme of this story.

• This story, like several others in this collection, is written from the point of view of the main character. What advantages does that provide a reader? What disadvantages?

• One of the things that fantasy and science fiction often do is make fun of our contemporary world. What does this story suggest about love and romance in today's world?

• Write a companion to this same story from Lauren's point of view.

FOURTH OF JULY

• What does the conversation among the three teen-agers tell us about their characters? Are they troublemakers, goody-goodies, or what? What kinds of students would you expect them to be in school?

• Did you want Chuck to throw the M-80 into Sager's car? What might have happened if he had done that? Why do you think Chuck didn't toss the firecracker into the car?

• How does the occasion of the Fourth of July contribute to the outcome of the story? How is the date symbolic?

• Have Chuck's actions evened things with Sager? How does Chuck feel about what he did with the gas?

• Add another scene to the story by describing Chuck's thoughts as he later sits with Kate and watches the fireworks explode over their heads.

• Describe Sager's reactions when his car runs out of gas. Will he vow revenge on Chuck or will he consider the score evened?

THREE PEOPLE AND TWO SEATS

• In what ways are Kenny and Brian typical kids?

• Why do the boys find it difficult to believe that Dave is a teacher?

• What is the purpose of Dave's bus ride? Why does he need a vacation so badly?

• How much of Dave's conflict is caused by kids in school, how much is caused by society in general, and how much of it is caused by his own expectations?

• By the time the bus reaches Gander, Dave has made a decision. How do you know what his decision is, and what led him to that decision?

• How important an influence does the Newfoundland location have on the outcome of this story? What does the setting on the bus itself contribute to the conflict and to the atmosphere of the story?

• Write the letter Dave might eventually write to the school board, stating the reasons for his resignation.

AN ORDINARY WOMAN

• What has Caren done? Why has she run away?

• Why is Mrs. Brooks changing the lock? How does she feel about what she's doing? How can she say she cares about her daughter when she's locking Caren out of the house?

• Do you think Mrs. Brooks has failed as a mother? What do you think caused the problems between her and her daughter?

• In what ways is Mrs. Brooks "an ordinary woman"? In what ways is she weak; in what ways strong?

• The entire story takes place in just a few minutes early one morning, but we also learn about several incidents from the past. What do we learn about the past and how does Greene accomplish that?

• We hear from Mrs. Brooks how she feels, but we don't know the story from Caren's side. Write Caren's side of the story, explaining how she feels about what she's done and how she feels about her mother.

THE GIFT-GIVING

• What makes the members of this family so close?

• Which do you think was the best gift of all? Why do you think so?

• In what ways is this story different from the others in this collection?

• How does the setting contribute to the mystery and the magical feeling of this story?

• What is the tone of this story and how does Joan Aiken create that tone?

• On a map of the world, locate as many places as you can that are mentioned in the story—e.g. Paris, Damascus, Hangku. . . .

• Using the same kind of storytelling style as Aiken, write a description of a magical place you can imagine.

SHE

• Why does Gogi read so much science fiction, and why does she do it in the bathroom?

• What are the differences between Linda's and Gogi's reactions to Dorine? What changes has Dorine's entrance into their home caused in their lives?

• The events are described from Gogi's point of view. How likely is it that Dorine is as nasty as Gogi thinks she is? What specific evidence does Gogi present to justify her negative feelings?

• Gogi says that Dorine won this skirmish. How will the outcome of this event affect the future relationship between Gogi and her stepmother?

• What expressions and feelings of the characters are possibly characteristic of people from the West Indies?

• Write a diary entry that Dorine might write on this evening, showing how she feels about the way she's been accepted by Linda and Gogi and how she feels about the way Gogi is acting on this particular evening.

IN THE HEAT

• It's not often that teen-agers see things from a parent's point of view. From what Richy's father says and thinks, what conclusions can you draw about his personality? What positive fatherly characteristics does he reveal? What flaws does he have? What makes him realistic?

• What do you learn about Richy? How is he like his father?

• What is the connection between the narrator's father and the present situation? How does the setting contribute to the atmosphere as well as to the theme of the story?

• Death is one of the saddest events we can experience. How does Cormier convey the sadness in this story? In what way is the story uplifting?

• Notice how Cormier employs several metaphors of violence—e.g. "The sun now is hemorrhaging to death . . . ," and "My heart is Hiroshima. . . ." What effect do they have on the tone of this story? How do they contrast with the quiet of the funeral home?

• What memories—pleasant or unpleasant—about one or both of your parents do you hold from your childhood or recent years that you will probably always remember? Write about one of those memories.

THE COLLECTION AS A WHOLE

• Of the teen-agers in "I, Hungry Hannah Cassandra Glen . . . ," "May I Have Your Autograph?," "Midnight Snack," "Priscilla and the Wimps," "Welcome," "Turmoil in a Blue and Beige Bedroom," "Three People and Two Seats," and

"She," which one is the most fun to be with? Which one is the most unusual individual? The most mature? The best student? The most fragile? The least sophisticated? The most unforgettable? The least interesting? Give evidence to support your opinions in each case.

• In most literature the main character changes as a result of something that happens in the story. (Remember that in some cases the change is only an insight into a problem the character has been struggling with.) Go back over the stories you have read and determine how each main character changed by the end of the story. Note if the change is for the better or worse or if there is no significant change at all.

• What human values are illustrated as being important in "Welcome," "Fourth of July," "An Ordinary Woman," "The Gift-Giving," and "In the Heat"?

• What incident do you think is the climax in each of the following stories: "Midnight Snack," "Pigeon Humor," "Welcome," "Future Tense," "Fourth of July," and "She"?

• Compare and contrast the mother in "An Ordinary Woman" with the father in "In the Heat" in terms of their concern for their child, their sensitivity to what has happened, their success as a parent, and their probable future relationship with their child.

• Which story aroused the most emotions in you? How did the story do that?

• Which story do you think you will remember the longest? Why do you think so?

• Write a short story of your own in which you use the same format or a similar style as that which is used in any one of the stories in this collection.

• Write your opinion of one of these stories and send it to the author (in care of the publisher).

• How does this collection compare to other collections of short stories you have had to read for school assignments?

What did you like about it? What didn't you like? Send your responses to the editor.

• Make a collection of stories you like from various sources. Share them with your friends. Publish your own collection.